Chase Calloway

*New York Times, USA Today & Wall Street Journal
bestselling author*
Sandi Lynn

Chase Calloway

Copyright © 2018 Sandi Lynn Romance, LLC

All rights reserved. No part of this publication may be reproduced, distributed, or transmitted in any form or by any means, including photocopying, recording, or other electronic or mechanical methods without the prior written permission of the publisher.

This is a work of fiction. Names, characters, places and incidents are the products of the authors imagination or are used fictitiously. Any resemblance to actual events, locales, or persons, living or dead, is entirely coincidental.

Photo by Wong Sim
Model: Lucas Bloms
Cover Design by: Sara Eirew @ Sara Eirew Photography

Editing by B.Z. Hercules

Mission Statement

Sandi Lynn Romance

*Providing readers with romance novels that will whisk them away
to another world and from the daily grind of life – one book at a time.*

Books by Sandi Lynn

If you haven't already done so, please check out my other books. Escape from reality and into the world of romance. I'll take you on a journey of love, pain, heartache and happily ever afters.

Millionaires:
The Forever Series (Forever Black, Forever You, Forever Us, Being Julia, Collin, A Forever Christmas, A Forever Family)
Love, Lust & A Millionaire (Wyatt Brothers, Book 1)
Love, Lust & Liam (Wyatt Brothers, Book 2)
Lie Next To Me (A Millionaire's Love, Book 1)
When I Lie with You (A Millionaire's Love, Book 2)
Then You Happened (Happened Series, Book 1)
Then We Happened (Happened Series, Book 2)
His Proposed Deal
A Love Called Simon
The Seduction of Alex Parker
Something About Lorelei
One Night In London
The Exception
Corporate A$$
A Beautiful Sight
The Negotiation
Defense
Playing The Millionaire
#Delete
Carter Grayson (Redemption Series, Book One)
Behind His Lies

Second Chance Love:
Remembering You
She Writes Love
Love In Between (Love Series, Book 1)
The Upside of Love (Love Series, Book 2)

Sports:
Lightning

Table of Contents

Chapter One 2
Chapter Two 9
Chapter Three 14
Chapter Four 19
Chapter Five 25
Chapter Six 33
Chapter Seven 40
Chapter Eight 45
Chapter Nine 49
Chapter Ten 54
Chapter Eleven 60
Chapter Twelve 66
Chapter Thirteen 71
Chapter Fourteen 77
Chapter Fifteen 81
Chapter Sixteen 87
Chapter Seventeen 93
Chapter Eighteen 100
Chapter Nineteen 107
Chapter Twenty 113
Chapter Twenty-One 117
Chapter Twenty-Two 124
Chapter Twenty-Three 130
Chapter Twenty-Four 136
Chapter Twenty-Five 143
Chapter Twenty-Six 150
Chapter Twenty-Seven 159

Chapter Twenty-Eight 165
Chapter Twenty-Nine 172
Chapter Thirty 178
Chapter Thirty-One 184
Chapter Thirty-Two 190
Chapter Thirty-Three 196
Chapter Thirty-Four 203
Chapter Thirty-Five 209
Chapter Thirty-Six 218
Chapter Thirty-Seven 225
Chapter Thirty-Eight 231
Chapter Thirty-Nine 238
Chapter Forty 244
Chapter Forty-One 253
Chapter Forty-Two 260
Chapter Forty-Three 265
Chapter Forty-Four 273
About the Author 277

Chapter One

Kinsley

Have you ever just wanted to run away from your life and move somewhere where nobody knew you? Not one single person? A place where you could start fresh and reinvent yourself? Your life? Your dreams? That was something I'd thought about since I was a little girl, and finally, I'd done it.

A nervousness settled inside me as I boarded the plane to California and took my seat. I needed to get as far away from Berkshire, Indiana as I could. My heart hurt, and I felt broken inside. Every emotion I could feel, I did. I sighed as I clutched the small white pillow to my chest and stared out the window at the runway that would take me away from this miserable place. I should have done this the minute I turned twenty years old, but I wasn't financially prepared at the time. By the time I was, when I was twenty-three, I met Henry, and he gave me a reason to stay. I should have known better. But this so-called thing everyone likes to say is love kept me from doing what I'd dreamt of ever since I was a child.

****

Eight Hours Earlier

I awoke with a smile on my face. Today was my boyfriend Henry's birthday. I got the day off from the greasy diner I worked at so I could plan something special for him. I'd made reservations at the Alpines, a fancy a la carte steakhouse that we'd talked about going to since the day they opened. I had these reservations for over a month because that was how far in advance they booked up. I hopped out of bed, showered, got dressed, and headed to Henry's favorite bakery to buy him his favorite cherry turnovers and coffee. He didn't know I had the day off from work. I wanted it to be a surprise and to be the best birthday he'd ever had.

I quietly inserted the key into the lock and slowly opened the door to his apartment, tiptoeing to the kitchen, where I set the bag of turnovers and the cups of coffee down on the counter. I arranged one of the cherry turnovers on a plate and stuck one candle in the middle. After lighting it, I carefully walked to his bedroom and opened the door. My heart started racing as I stood there and stared at him with his arms around another woman. And not just any other woman, but my best friend, Krista.

"What the fuck!" I shouted.

Henry jumped out of bed while Krista sat up, holding the sheet up to cover her naked body.

"Kinsley. What are you doing here?" he nervously spoke.

"Kinsley, I can explain," Krista spoke as she held up her hand.

I swallowed hard as tears streamed down my face and a sick feeling erupted inside me.

"Kinsley." Henry pulled on a pair of shorts and began to walk towards me.

I had so much to say, to scream, to shout, but nothing would come out of my mouth. I put my hand up in front of Henry to stop him from coming any closer.

"Don't," I managed to speak in a shaky voice.

He stopped dead in his tracks.

"Baby, please. This isn't what it looks like," he spoke.

I shook my head in disbelief as he stood there and tried to lie his way out of it.

"This isn't what it looks like?" I spoke through gritted teeth. "I walk into your bedroom and find you in bed, totally naked and holding my best friend! How long has this been going on?" I shouted as my eyes met Krista's. "TELL ME!" I screamed.

"Just a couple of times," she spoke. "I'm so sorry, Kinsley. I didn't mean for it to happen."

"Yeah, baby. It was only a couple times thing. Please believe me," Henry spoke. "It meant absolutely nothing. I promise, nothing."

"How could the both of you do this to me?" I asked as the tears wouldn't stop falling. "Henry, how could you?" I slowly shook my head as I stared into his lying eyes.

"Kinsley, I—" he started to speak.

I looked down at the turnover, blew out the candle, and proceeded to throw the plate at him. He ducked as it smashed against the wall.

"You two are dead to me." I pointed at both of them. "Do you understand? DEAD!" I turned around and stormed out of the bedroom.

"Kinsley, wait!" Krista yelled as she came after me.

I grabbed my purse from the kitchen, and as I was walking

to the door, she grabbed hold of my hand to try and stop me.

"Don't do this. I'm so sorry. I didn't mean for it to happen," she begged as she fell to the floor with a tight grip on my hand.

"You sleep with my boyfriend, the man I'd been dating for over a year, and you have the nerve to tell me not to do this!" I shouted. "Well guess what, Krista, the two of you can have each other and you can both rot in Hell."

"Kinsley, baby, me and you need to talk about this like adults," Henry spoke. "It was a mistake."

"Adults?" I glared at him. "You're not a man. You're a fucking coward and far from ever being an adult. Happy birthday, Henry. I hope you get everything you want, and by the looks of it, you already have."

I jerked my hand from Krista's grip, flew out the door, got into my car, and sped away. I pulled over on the side of the road about five miles from Henry's apartment. My hands tightly gripped the steering wheel as my forehead fell onto it. I felt as if I was having a panic attack. I couldn't breathe, and now, I knew what I needed to do. I pulled my phone from my purse and dialed Jimmy.

"Hey, Kinsley, what's up?"

"Do you still want to buy my car?" I asked.

"Yeah. Sure. You're selling?"

"Yes. Give me a couple of hours and I'll drop it off. I want four thousand cash. Is that enough time for you to get the money?"

"Yeah. No problem. I'll go to the bank now. What's going

on?"

"I just don't need it anymore."

"Did something happen?" he asked.

"I'll see you soon." I ended the call.

I drove to the bank and closed down my bank account. Then I drove home, and as soon as I stepped through the front door, I found my mom passed out on the couch. Rolling my eyes, I ran to my bedroom, threw as many of my things that would fit in my suitcase, and headed back to the living area.

"Mom?" I lightly shook her.

"Not now, Kinsley," she moaned.

Shaking my head, I went into the kitchen, grabbed a pen and a piece of paper from the drawer, and wrote her a note.

"Mom, I'm leaving. I can't stay here anymore. This isn't the life I want. Don't worry about me and I really hope you get your shit together someday."

Kinsley

I placed the note on the coffee table in front of the couch she was passed out on and walked out the front door, pulling my suitcase behind me. As I drove to Jimmy's shop, I called an Uber to meet me there.

"What's going on, Kinsley?" Jimmy asked.

"I'm leaving town. I can't stay here anymore," I spoke as I took the cash from his hands and handed him the keys to my car.

"What about Henry? Does he know?"

"Henry is fucking Krista, so I'm positive he won't care."

"Gee, I'm sorry." He scratched his head. "Where are you going?"

"I don't know yet."

"And what about your mom?"

"She'll be fine. It'll probably be a couple of days before she notices I'm gone anyway."

The Uber pulled up and rolled down the passenger side window.

"Are you Kinsley?" he asked.

"Yeah." I nodded.

I walked over to my car and took my suitcase from the trunk.

"Thanks, Jimmy."

"You're welcome, Kinsley. Good luck and stay safe." He hugged me.

"I will." I gave him a small smile and shoved the money he gave me into my purse.

As I was sitting in the back of the car, my phone was being blown up by calls and text messages from Henry. I rolled down the window and tossed it out in the middle of the highway.

"Lady, why did you do that?" the Uber driver asked.

"I don't need it anymore. That part of my life is gone."

He dropped me off at the airport and I wheeled my suitcase up to the reservations desk.

"How can I help you?" the friendly brunette asked.

"I need a one-way ticket to California. Next flight out if possible."

"You're in luck. The next flight leaves in two hours and there are two seats left." She smiled.

Chapter Two

Chase

"Oh, Chase," Rachel moaned. "You—are—amazing."

"Yes, darling, I know." I smiled at her as I buttoned my shirt.

"Do you have to go already?" she asked.

"Unfortunately, adulting calls. I need to get to the office or my father is going to have my head."

"Call me later?" She seductively smiled.

"Of course." I winked as I grabbed my suitcoat and walked out the door.

I climbed into my black convertible Aston Martin and sped down the highway like I owned it. As I was jamming to my favorite tunes with a grin on my face, my secretary, Lexi, facetimed me.

"Morning, beautiful." I smiled.

"Chase, where are you? Your father is looking for you."

"I'm on my way. Tell him I was up late finishing the coding for the new computer system."

"Did you finish it?"

"Not yet, sweetheart, but I will before he finds me." I smirked. "Make sure my coffee is on my desk because I need it."

"You know I hate lying to him. I could lose my job," she whispered as she moved her face closer to the phone.

"You're not going to lose your job, darling. And besides, you're not lying to him. Like I said, it'll be done before he finds me. I'll see you soon." I hit the end button.

The wind blew across my face as I gunned it and turned up the radio as loud as it would go. I pulled into the parking garage of Calloway Tech, parked in my parking space, and entered the back of the building. I stepped inside an empty office, took the flash drive from the inside pocket of my suitcoat, and inserted it. "Okay. Let's do this." I smiled as I began typing. Fifteen minutes later, and it was done. That was me. Always putting shit off to the last second. I pulled the flash drive out, shut down the computer, and headed to my father's office.

"Well, hello there." I grinned at the beautiful brunette sitting outside his office. "You're not Audrey." I took a seat on the edge of her desk.

"Hello." She bit down on her bottom lip. "I'm a temp. Audrey is out ill."

"Ah. Sorry to hear that, but lucky for us, you were able to fill in for her. Chase Calloway." I extended my hand.

"Isabella." She smiled as she placed her well-manicured hand in mine.

"Chase!" my father yelled as he opened his office door. "Get in here."

"It was nice to make your acquaintance. Maybe we can grab a drink or three after work."

"I'd love that," she swooned.

Walking into my father's office, I shut the door, took the flash drive out of my pocket, and set it on his desk.

"There you go, Dad. I told you I'd have it finished by today."

"You were up all night finishing it?" His eye narrowed at me.

"Of course." I tucked my hands in my pants pockets.

"Isn't that the same suit you were wearing yesterday?" he asked with suspicion.

"This?" I looked down. "Of course not. Do you know how many of these suits I own?"

"Really?" He glared at me as he turned his computer screen around. "It says here you were boozing it up last night at the strip club. That is you? Correct?" His brow arched as he pointed to the picture of me with a drink in one hand and a half naked Rachel in the other.

"So what? I needed to unwind before I finished the program. The only thing that matters is it's done and ready to go. Right?" I raised my shoulders.

"Get out of here. I'm sure you need some coffee." He smirked.

"Thanks, Dad. I'll see you later." I began to walk out of his office.

"Chase?" he called out.

"Yes?"

"Stay away from my temp."

"Well, Dad." I grinned. "You sly dog. Keeping the temp all to yourself?"

"For fucks sake, son, get the hell out of here and get to work." He shook his head.

Walking out of his office and past Isabella's desk, I gave her a wink and smile. I loved beautiful women and she was definitely beautiful. I walked into my office and threw my briefcase down on my chair.

"Did you see your father?" Lexi asked as she followed me in.

"Yes, Lexi, you can relax. All is good." I grinned. "So, what's on the agenda for today?" I asked as I picked up my coffee cup and took a soothing sip.

"You have a meeting at one o'clock with Lux security. They want an update on the app for their systems."

"Shit. I don't have an update yet. No worries, hold all my calls and I don't want to be disturbed. I have an update to get ready."

"Sure thing, Chase. By the way, you have that fundraiser to go to tonight."

"What fundraiser?" I glanced at her.

"The one to which your father is sending you to represent the company for him."

"Ah yes. I forgot about that. Thanks for reminding me."

Chase Calloway

I sat down at my desk, picked up my phone, and dialed my father's office number.

"Good morning, Calloway Tech, how can I help you?"

"Hello, Isabella, it's Chase Calloway. How would you like to attend a fundraiser with me tonight? There will be free food and drinks among other delicious things."

"I would love to go with you."

"Excellent. Send me your address and I will pick you up at seven o'clock."

"I look forward to it, Mr. Calloway."

I ended the call with a smile on my face.

"Hey, bro. How did it go with Rachel last night?" Steven walked in my office and playfully punched my arm.

"No complaints." I smirked. "By the way, stop taking pics of me and posting it on your social media. My father saw it and he wasn't happy."

"Come on, Chase." He laughed. "How else do you think you've been named L.A.'s sexiest and most eligible bachelor?" He grinned.

Chapter Three

Kinsley

As soon as my feet hit the pavement of Los Angeles, California, I stopped and stared at the beautiful sight before me. The palm trees, the mountains, and the hustle and bustle of people all around. I took in a deep breath as a man approached me.

"You need a cab, lady?" he asked.

"Actually, I do."

"Right this way." He smiled.

I climbed into the back and the cab driver looked at me through his rearview mirror.

"Where to?"

"I don't really know." I bit down on my bottom lip.

His brow arched as he turned and glanced at me.

"Have you never been to California?" he asked.

"No. I just decided this morning that I was moving here."

"Wow. Okay. So, I take it you don't have a plan?"

"No. It was rather an impulsive decision. Well, actually, it's something I've dreamed of ever since I was a kid."

"Ah, something or someone pushed you here before you had the chance to really think about it?"

"Yeah. You could say that. I came here to reinvent myself. Start my life over."

"Well, then, welcome to the City of Angels." He smiled. "I'm Reece, by the way." He held back his hand.

"I'm Kinsley."

"Nice to meet you, Kinsley. Tell you what. My cousin owns the Coral Sands Motel in Hollywood. I'll take you there and make sure you get a room. Rates are cheap. You can start there and then figure things out."

"Thanks, Reece. I appreciate it." I kindly smiled.

He pulled up to the curb of the Coral Sands Motel. After I paid him his fare, he took my suitcase out of the trunk and walked me through the door.

"Reece!" an older woman from behind the counter exclaimed. "What brings you in here?" She smiled as she hugged him.

"Madeline, this is Kinsley. Kinsley, this is my cousin Madeline."

"Nice to meet you." I extended my hand.

"Kinsley just moved here, spur of the moment type of thing. She needs a room."

"Ah. I see." Madeline smiled. "I can definitely help you with that."

"You're in good hands, Kinsley," Reece spoke. "Here's my card. Whenever you need a ride, call me."

"Thank you, Reece. I will." I took the card from his hand.

"Good luck. Hope to see you again soon."

I handed Madeline my driver's license and credit card.

"The rate is $90 a night and you will be in room 24, which is on the 2nd level. If you need anything at all, please let me know."

"Thank you. Do you know where the closest phone store is around here? Preferably within walking distance?"

"There's actually one about two blocks from here, but I'm afraid they're already closed. They'll open again tomorrow morning at ten."

"Okay. Thank you."

I pulled my suitcase behind me out the doors to the courtyard and up the steps to room 24. Once I was inside, I let go of my suitcase and looked around. I was surprised at how nice and clean the room was. The walls were colored in yellow with a double-size bed, two nightstands that each housed tall lamps, a small round table with two chairs, a TV, and a microwave and mini fridge that sat in the corner. I pulled the drapes closed and went into the bathroom for a bath. I was exhausted and needed to relax and think about my next move.

As I lay there in the hot water, I thought about the events of today. My eyes swelled with tears as the scene of Krista and Henry played over and over in my mind. Had I moved here a year ago like I wanted to, I would have already been settled. Damn Henry for coming into my life. I kept telling myself that everything happens for a reason. It was what I'd told myself since I was sixteen years old and worked for Mrs. Buckley at the antique shop. It was what she told me.

"Kinsley, everything that happens to us in life happens for a reason. There are no coincidences. Never forget that. Every event and situation will only make you stronger for the next challenge."

And she was right. I was stronger because of my childhood and life. She was like a mother to me. This sweet, frail seventy-year-old woman whose life was her antique shop. Her husband passed away when she was fifty-five and they never had any children. I worked for her for six years and saved every penny I made for when this day would come. I didn't make very much, but it didn't matter because Mrs. Buckley was like family to me and I loved working for her. The year she died, I'd finally had enough money saved to leave Indiana, but then I met Henry, and somehow, he swept me off my feet. I thought maybe he'd make my life better in Berkshire. Since I decided to stay, I ended up taking a job at Freddy's diner. A grease pit where I worked for a year as a waitress, being treated like shit and getting groped by the pigs that dined there frequently. But I could handle them.

Maybe finding out about Krista and Henry was a blessing in disguise. Who knew and only time would tell. I was here now and today was the start of my new life and I would never let another man deter me from my plans. In fact, I was staying away from all men for a long time.

After my bath, I changed into my pajamas, grabbed my laptop, and climbed into bed. First things first, I needed to find a job ASAP. Even though I had quite a bit of money saved, it wouldn't last long without a job, especially with what things cost in California. After an hour of searching and just finally applying to a temp agency, I decided to pull up apartments for rent. Where did I want to live? I didn't know. I knew nothing about California. My eyes kept closing, so I shut down my laptop and went to sleep.

Chapter Four

Chase

I slowly opened my eyes as the sun pierced them through the blinds.

"Ah." I placed my arm over my eyes as I turned my head.

"Good morning, handsome." Isabella smiled as she stroked my chest. "You were amazing last night."

"Why, thank you. You weren't so bad yourself."

I climbed out of bed and headed to the bathroom.

"You can get dressed now and go," I shouted from the bathroom. "I'm sure you have plans today."

"Actually, I don't," she spoke.

"Well, I do." I smiled as I emerged from the bathroom. "I have some waves to catch with a couple buddies of mine."

"Super cool. Can I come?" she asked in her way too high-pitched voice.

"Sorry, darling. Men only." I winked as I picked up her clothes off the floor and tossed them at her.

"When can I see you again, Chase?"

"Well, I'm sure I'll be seeing you at the office on Monday."

I walked out of the bedroom and into the kitchen for some coffee.

"But we'll both be working. I meant when can we go out again?"

"Oh." I turned and looked at her. "I'm not sure. I have a busy weekend. I'll be in touch."

She stood in the middle of my kitchen and began to cry. For Christ sakes.

"Why are you crying, Isabella?"

"Because I get the feeling that we won't be seeing each other again and I really like you."

Rolling my eyes, I walked over to her and gripped her shoulders.

"You've only known me twenty-four hours. That clearly isn't enough time to decide if you like someone."

"So, you're saying you don't like me?" The tears streamed down her face.

"No. No. I didn't say that. It's just I'm a very busy man and I see a variety of women. It seems to me that a girl like you is looking for some type of relationship."

"So?"

I sighed. "I'm not a relationship type of person. We had fun and everything and now it's time to part ways."

God, how I hated explaining this to women.

"So, you used me?" Her teary eyes turned to anger.

"Sweetheart, we used each other. It was all in fun."

"But I thought you really liked me."

"I do, but not in a relationship type of way. Would you like some coffee before you leave?"

"Ugh. You're just like all the other douchebag men out there in the world!" she shouted as she turned on her heels and headed towards the front door.

"I do believe I'm one of a kind," I shouted as the front door slammed.

Shaking my head, I picked up my coffee cup and took a sip. After popping two aspirins with a shot of scotch, I showered, grabbed my surfboard, and headed down to the beach.

"Bro, what took you so long?" Steven asked.

"Yeah, we were getting worried something happened to you," Alex spoke.

"I was dealing with a little problem named Isabella."

"Isn't that your dad's temp?" Steven asked.

"Yes."

The three of us put our boards in the water.

"Dude, she's one smokin' hot ass chick. What was the problem?"

"She didn't want to leave, and she wanted to know when we're seeing each other again."

Alex laughed. "Obviously, she doesn't know a thing about Chase Calloway."

"She does now, and she left crying. I hate when they do that."

"Just another broken heart amongst all the others in the sea of Chase Calloway." Alex smiled.

"She'll be fine once she gets me out of her system," I spoke.

Steven and Alex were my best friends. My bros. My buds. We'd been friends since freshman year in high school. All three of us grew up rich and we all attended Stanford University. Steven and I obtained degrees in Computer Science while Alex pursued a degree in Biochemical Engineering and now worked for his father's pharmaceutical company. We were roommates in an off-campus luxury three-bedroom apartment during our college years. In between studies, we partied as if our lives would end tomorrow. Hell, we still did. Some things never changed. Except for Alex. He met Lindsey and fell in love. She changed him, and Steven and I didn't like it.

We were out and had just caught the last wave that hit. The three of us were chilling with our boards in the water, waiting for the next one, when Alex said he had something to tell us.

"I'm going to ask Lindsey to marry me and I wanted the two of you to know first," he spoke.

"Dude, you sure you want that?" Steven asked.

"Of course I want that. I love her."

"You two already live together. Why do you need to get married?" I asked.

"Because it's the next step in our relationship. I love her more than anything in this world and I want her to be my wife. Why is that so hard for the two of you to understand?"

"Because it's not natural. Marriages don't last, dear friend, and you know it," I spoke. "Besides, who wants to be tied down to the same pussy for the rest of their life?"

"I do, and you know why? Because for the hundredth time, I love her, and I can't imagine my life without her. But the two of you wouldn't know anything about that because all you care about is getting drunk and fucking a different woman every damn night."

"And? What's wrong with that? You were one of us once. Don't forget that!" I pointed at him.

"Yeah, bro," Steven spoke. "You were just as bad as we were."

"Yeah, the key word being 'was.' But all that changed when I met Lindsey. Nah, forget it. You two will never understand." He waved his hand. "I thought you'd be happy for me. You're my best friends."

"Look, man, I'm sorry," I spoke. "We are happy for you. We know you're happy with Lindsey and she's a great girl. We just don't want to see you get hurt."

"I'm not going to get hurt. I love her and she loves me."

"Love fades, bro," Steven said.

I turned and splashed water at him.

"Not ours. I'm asking her to marry me tonight. In fact, I'm going to head back to shore. I want to make sure everything is perfect," Alex spoke.

"I'm done anyway," I spoke. "You coming, Steven?"

"I guess." He sighed.

****

"He's making a mistake," I spoke as I poured two glasses of scotch.

"No shit," Steven spoke as he took the glass from my hand.

"Why the hell would anyone want to commit to one single person for the rest of their life? Everyone knows it won't last. They just try to convince themselves that it will for some kind of temporary happiness. My father is the perfect example of that."

"I don't know, bro." Steven shook his head. "Obviously, Lindsey put a spell on him."

"I agree." I held up my glass. "No woman will ever do that to me. I don't and will never give anyone that kind of power. Fuck no."

"Yeah, bro! Fuck no!" He tapped his glass against mine with a smile.

"I need to get laid and drunk," I spoke as I finished off my scotch.

"Me too, man."

"Shall we hit the Skybar tonight?" I asked with a grin.

"God, I love the women at the Skybar. I'm going to go home and take a nap first."

"Sweet dreams, bro. I'll pick you up around eight o'clock," I spoke.

Chapter Five

Kinsley

For the first time in my life, I woke up feeling free. Free from the bondage that kept me tied to Berkshire. I lay in bed as my mind woke up and started going crazy with everything that I had to do. I pulled a pad of paper and pen out of the drawer in the nightstand and began to write down my goals and my tasks. I'd always found that if I had everything in my head written down, I could complete each to do item with ease and no stress.

1. Go to bank and open an account.
2. Go to phone store and buy a new phone.
3. Look for an apartment.
4. Look for a job.
5. Look for a car.
6. Go to the beach and let the water sweep over my feet.

I tore the paper from the pad and put it in my purse. After I showered and got dressed, I opened the curtains to let the beautiful California sun into my room. A smile swept over my face as I stood there and stared at the palm trees that gracefully danced as the light wind took its lead.

I left my room and walked across the street to a coffee house and grabbed a coffee and a scone to kick off my day. I walked the couple blocks, found a phone store, and got myself a brand new iPhone and a new number. Because I was a new customer to the provider, I only had to pay forty dollars for the phone. Things were already starting to look up. I pulled Reece's card from my purse and dialed his number.

"Reece here," he answered.

"Hi, Reece, it's Kinsley."

"Kinsley, my girl. How was your first night in California?"

"It was good. Thanks. You said to call you if I needed a cab. Well, I need a cab. Are you available?"

"I'm just dropping off someone now. Are you at the motel?"

"Yes."

"I can be there in about twenty minutes. Hang tight."

"Thanks, Reece."

I ended the call, walked back to the motel, and sipped my coffee and ate my scone while I waited for him. It had been twenty minutes on the dot when he pulled up to the curb.

"Where to, Kinsley?" He smiled.

"Well, I need to buy a car. Are the dealerships open on Saturdays?"

"Yep. They're open until two o'clock, so you have plenty of time. There's a used car dealership not too far from here. Wanna check it out?"

"Yeah, I do." I nodded.

I glanced on his dashboard and saw a picture of a beautiful

woman with long dark hair and three children, all boys. A picture I didn't notice yesterday.

"Is that your family?" I asked as I pointed to the picture.

"They sure are." He proudly grinned. "That's my wife Nadia and our boys, Samuel, Jacob, and Luke."

"Names from the Bible." I smiled.

"Yes. That's right. They are my world. Samuel is ten, Jacob is eight, and Luke is four. We planned on stopping after Jacob, but God had other plans for us."

"They're beautiful."

"Thanks. What about you? Do you have any family?" he asked.

"Not really. I have a mom back in Indiana. That's about it."

Reece could hear the somberness in my voice, and as much as he wanted to know why I suddenly hopped on a plane and moved here, he didn't ask. He was a nice guy. Early forties, short black hair, brown eyes, and an overall good attitude about life.

"Hey, Reece, can I ask you something?"

"Sure, Kinsley. You can ask me anything."

"Why do you drive a cab?"

He let out a laugh and looked at me through his rearview mirror.

"I drive a cab because it's in my blood. It's my company. My father handed it over to me when he retired. Plus, I love people. Everyone has a different story to tell, but in the end, we're all the same."

"Nice." I smiled.

He pulled into the used car lot and walked around with me while I looked at cars.

"Hello there." A jolly older man approached us. "Looking for a car?"

"I am. My name is Kinsley." I held out my hand.

"Nice to meet you, Kinsley. I'm Bill. So, tell me what you're looking for?"

"Anything that is reliable and will cost me no more than four thousand dollars out the door."

"Okay. I have just the car for you." He grinned. "Follow me."

He led us over to a silver Ford Focus.

"This here is a 2010 Focus. It's the cheapest car I have on the lot and probably one of the most reliable. It has a hundred and eight thousand miles on it. But don't let that scare you." He put up his hand. "Under the hood is all pretty much new parts. It runs like a charm."

"How much?" I arched my brow at him.

"This one is fifty-five hundred, but since you seem like such a sweet girl, I'll give it to you for five grand. Like I said, it's the cheapest car I have."

"And like I said, no more than four grand out the door. Did I mention I was paying for the car in cash?" I cocked my head innocently at him.

"Cash? Do you have four grand with you now?" His brow raised.

"Yes." I grinned.

"Congratulations on your new vehicle, Kinsley." The corners of his mouth curved into a wide smile. "Step inside my office and we can fill out the paperwork."

I gave Reece a hug and thanked him for being so kind.

"Thank you for everything, Reece. This truly is the city of Angels." I smiled.

"You're welcome, Kinsley. Now that you have that car, don't be a stranger. I'd like to have you over for a barbeque to meet my wife and kids."

"I'd love that."

"I'll text you, okay?"

"Okay." I smiled.

After signing the papers, Bill handed me the keys to my car. I climbed inside and ran my hand over the soft black cloth seats with a smile on my face. Pulling out the paper from my purse, I checked off three items on my list. The bank would have to wait until Monday since they closed at noon and it was already one thirty. I punched in the address to the motel into google maps and followed the directions back, missing a turn and ending up in downtown Los Angeles. I was starving, so I decided to grab a bite to eat before attempting to find my way back to the motel. After pulling into a parking space, I got out of my car and walked along the street, stumbling across a restaurant called Cabbage Patch. It sounded interesting, so I stepped inside and ordered a BLTA sandwich and an order of fries. While I was eating, I finished setting up my phone, and as I connected my new email address to it, I received one from the temp agency I applied to last night, asking me to call them as soon as possible.

"TeamOne staffing agency. How can I help you?" A friendly voice answered.

"Hi, this is Kinsley Davis. I just received an email asking me to call you as soon as possible."

"Just one moment, Miss Davis. Let me see who is handling your application. That would be Miss Johnson. Hold please and I'll put you through to her."

"Miss Davis, this is Charlotte Johnson speaking. Thank you for your prompt response. Is it possible for you to come in for an interview right now?"

"Umm. I'm out at the moment and I'm afraid I'm not dressed appropriately for an interview."

"Well, what are you wearing?" she asked.

"A maxi dress," I replied.

"Good enough for me. How soon can you get here?"

"I don't know. Where are you located?"

"2999 Overland Avenue, Suite 212, Los Angeles."

I hurried and typed the address into google maps while she rattled it off to me.

"According to my GPS, I can be there in fifteen minutes," I

spoke.

"Perfect. I'll be waiting."

I hurried and finished the last of my sandwich, got in my car, and carefully followed the directions to the TeamOne office. I couldn't believe this was happening. Pulling into a parking space, I climbed out of my car and walked through the large glass double doors.

"Miss Davis?" A dark-haired older woman smiled at me.

"Yes?"

"I'm Charlotte Johnson. Follow me up to my office."

Once we reached her office, I took the seat across from her desk as she took hers behind it.

"I was impressed with your resume and we would like you as part of TeamOne. We have a job available for you to start on Monday if you're interested."

"I'm very interested. Thank you. I didn't think temp agencies worked over the weekends."

"Normally, we don't. But when we have very important clients, we do anything we can to accommodate them. I will text you the address to the office building you'll be working at. The job will only be available for about eight weeks. When your time is close to expiring at that job, we will be working hard to place you somewhere else."

"Okay. Don't you need to interview me? Ask me my skills or any questions?"

"No. No. Trust me. Just by looking at you, I can already tell you're perfect for the job."

"Oh. Well, thank you."

"All of our other temps who would be perfect as well are already placed elsewhere, so we are kind of in a pickle and we can't afford to upset our client."

Chapter Six

Chase

My alarm was going off, and I sighed as I opened my eyes, grabbed my phone, and shut it down. If I didn't love the waves so much, I would be sleeping in for another two hours before heading into the office. The weekend was crazy fun but exhausting. Saturday night with Steven at the Skybar landed me in a hotel room with Sophie and last night's escapades didn't get me home until two a.m.

It was six a.m. before I officially climbed out of bed, grabbed my surfboard, and headed into the water. The number of sexy women that were already on the beach doing yoga in their tight as fuck pants and skimpy sports bras was enough to wake anybody up.

"Hello." I smiled as I passed by each one of them. "Beautiful way to start the day." I grinned as I stared at their perfectly shaped asses.

I threw my board into the water and paddled out, waiting for the waves to hit. The sun was rising as I sat on my board and stared at the beauty of it. The only real place I felt any kind of peace was out here, in the middle of the open water, letting the waves break over me. It wasn't too long before I was joined by others who felt the same way I did. A lot of people went to the gym to get their morning exercise in before starting their day, but not me. I got in my morning exercise by surfing and having sex. I saved the gym time for either midday or early evening after the office, depending on what my plans were. I surfed for about an hour and then headed back up to the house to shower and get ready for work.

"Good morning, Lexi." I grinned as I walked past her desk and into my office.

"Good morning, Chase," she spoke as she set my coffee down on the desk.

"How was your weekend?" I asked.

"It was good. Ben and I spent a couple of days in Napa."

"Ah. Got filthy drunk on all that wine?" I smirked.

"I wouldn't say filthy drunk." She grinned. "Don't forget you have a meeting with John Koppelinger at eleven o'clock."

"Thanks. I did forget. Is my father in yet?"

"Your father's been here since six a.m., and he wanted me to tell you that you are to be in his office the minute you get in."

"He and Penelope must be fighting again." I smiled. "One can only hope. I can't stand that wretched woman."

"That wretched woman is going to be your stepmother."

I shrugged. "Maybe not. I think dear old Dad is finally seeing her for who she really is. Anyway, thanks for the coffee. I'm going to head over to his office."

As I was walking down the hallway, I noticed a beautiful blonde sitting at the desk outside his office.

"Well." I smiled brightly as I stopped. "You aren't Isabella."

She looked up and her blue eyes pierced me.

"No. I'm Kinsley." She smiled.

"Kinsley." I gave a cunning grin. "What a beautiful name for an extraordinarily beautiful woman."

"Chase, get your ass in here!" my father shouted.

"As soon as I'm finished, I'll be back to properly introduce myself." I winked as I headed into his office and closed the door behind me. "Good morning, Dad. You seem a little on edge this morning. Everything okay?"

"No, Chase, everything is not okay. What was the one thing I told you to do?" he spoke in a stern authoritative voice.

"I don't know. You ask me to do a lot of things."

"For fucks sake. I specifically told you to stay away from the temp! Didn't I?"

"Oh. You mean Isabella?" I smiled.

"She quit, and I know you had something to do with it! You slept with her, didn't you?"

"Listen, Dad. I took her to the fundraiser. The one you," I pointed at him, "made me attend because you didn't want to. I didn't want to go alone, so I asked her to tag along. There was drinking involved and one thing led to another. I politely told her the next morning that it was a one-time thing. It's not my fault she couldn't handle it."

"You have a million women you could have asked! She was actually a very good temp."

"Please." I rolled my eyes. "She worked for you for one day. How could you possibly know if she was any good? Wait a minute. You two didn't—" I wiggled my fingers.

"Of course not! I'm engaged to Penelope!"

"Well, Dad, that never seemed to stop you before." I cocked my head.

He glared at me as he rested his hands on his desk and then shook his finger at me without saying a word. I could see the anger splayed across his face.

"Don't even try, Dad. You're the one who set specifications on who you want sitting outside your office, and now look, Kinsley out there is even more beautiful than Isabella. So actually, you can thank me."

"Thank you? For what?!" he loudly voiced.

"For the departure of Isabella. You're welcome."

"You literally have two seconds to get out of my sight before I disown you!"

"Fine." I put my hands up and walked out of his office, shutting the door behind me.

I looked at Kinsley, who sat there looking down with a grin on her face.

"You heard all of that?" I asked.

"Really only the part where he said he was going to disown you if you didn't get out of his office." She began to laugh.

"Don't mind him. He tends to get wound up over nothing. Anyway." I smiled as I extended my hand. "I'm Chase

Calloway, son of Dean Calloway."

"Kinsley Davis. It's a pleasure to meet you, Mr. Calloway." She smiled back as she placed her hand in mine, sending my cock twitching beyond control.

"Trust me." I cocked my head. "The pleasure is all mine."

"Now if you'll excuse me, I need to get back to work," she spoke as she got up from her seat, grabbed some files, and headed into my father's office.

"Of course. Enjoy your day."

I swallowed hard and placed my hand in my pocket as I walked back to my office. She stood about five feet eight with legs that were long and lean. Her hair was blonde, naturally blonde with loose waves at the ends that flowed perfectly over her shoulders. Her eyes were heightened by the arch of her perfectly manicured brows. The color of them wasn't your typical blue. They were more of an aquamarine color, the perfect mix of blue and green. Her slender jawline and perfectly shaped lips and nose made her face pure perfection. She captivated me and left me momentarily at a loss for words.

I let out a deep breath as I took a seat behind my desk.

"Hey, Chase," Steven spoke as he walked into my office. "I have—hey, are you okay?"

"I don't know. I think I just saw an angel."

He chuckled. "Who is it this time?"

"My dad's new temp. Her name is Kinsley Davis."

"Wait a minute. I thought your dad's new temp was

Isabella?"

"She quit." I waved my hand.

He rolled his eyes. "And I'm sure that had nothing to do with your rejection of her."

"Who cares. We're talking about Kinsley here. I want to go out with her. No, I take that back, I NEED to go out with her."

"You mean you NEED to fuck her," he spoke.

"Yeah. That too. Dad wasn't too happy about Isabella quitting. He just laid into me a few minutes ago."

"Then you better back off of Kinsley."

"No can do, man. I'll figure out a way to get to know her without compromising her job here. Plus, how long is she really going to be here? I'm sure Audrey will be back in a couple of days. I'll just wait until she gets back and Kinsley is no longer working here."

"Hey, Lexi, can you come in here for a minute?" Steven yelled from my office.

"Yes, Steven?"

"What's going on with Audrey? Does she have the flu or something?"

"No. They found some suspicious tumors on her uterus. She had to have a hysterectomy. It really happened so fast."

"So how long will she be out of the office?" I asked with great concern for my getting to know Kinsley.

"About eight weeks."

"For fucks sake." I shook my head.

"I don't understand?" Lexi narrowed her eye at me.

"I feel bad for my dad. I mean look, Isabella already quit after one day and now there's another new temp. God knows how long she'll last."

"Stay away from her and I'm sure she'll last the whole eight weeks." She smiled.

Steven let out a laugh.

"Don't you have work to do, Lexi?"

"Yes. Actually, I do."

"Great, now what am I supposed to do? There's no way in hell I'm waiting eight weeks," I spoke as I looked at Steven.

"I don't know, bro." He sighed. "Good luck with that one. By the way, I finished the Lexington program. Take a double look and let me know your thoughts."

"I will. Thanks, Steven."

Chapter Seven

Kinsley

Everything was happening so fast that I didn't have time to think about anything else, and for that, I was grateful. Excitement overtook me because I had an appointment after work to look at a furnished apartment that was for rent in Santa Monica right across from the water. The monthly rent wasn't listed, and from what I could tell by the pictures online, it looked nice. When I asked Mrs. Graham how much she was charging, she told me to come look at the apartment first and then we'd discuss the rent, which I found a little odd. I prayed that I liked it as much in person and it was in my price range, because all I wanted was a permanent place to call home.

I was sitting at my desk when Chase Calloway walked over.

"Hello there, Kinsley." He grinned as he planted himself on the edge of the desk.

"Hi. Can I help you with something?"

"Oh, darling, you can help me with a lot of things." His grin widened. "But, anyway, is he in there?" he asked as he pointed to the office door.

"No. He's in a meeting right now."

"Hmm. Okay. I'll have to catch him later. I wanted to ask

you if you would like to have dinner with me tonight. I would like to personally welcome you to Calloway Tech."

My brow arched as I stared into his blue eyes.

"No thank you. I have plans." I lightly smiled.

Chase cleared his throat as he stood up.

"Oh. Of course you do. A beautiful woman such as yourself certainly wouldn't be sitting home all alone." I caught him looking at my left hand. "I'm sure you and your boyfriend already have dinner plans."

I knew exactly what he was trying to find out, and if I didn't let him know that I was onto him, he'd probably think I was stupid.

"No." I shook my head.

"No what?"

"My boyfriend and I don't have dinner plans."

"Well, then you must have other plans with him."

"No." I smirked.

"No, you don't have any plans with him?"

"No. I have plans with myself. I don't have a boyfriend, Mr. Calloway."

"I see. Well, I can honestly say that I'm shocked. You're too beautiful not to be seeing someone."

"Thank you for the compliment. I appreciate it."

"You're welcome." The corners of his mouth curved up into

a smile. "By the way, just call me Chase. Mr. Calloway reminds me too much of my father." He sighed.

Just as Chase was about to say another word, his father walked up behind him and placed his hand on his shoulder.

"What are you doing, Chase?"

"Actually, Dad, I was looking for you."

"I'm here, so come into my office," he spoke.

"We'll talk soon." Chase winked as he followed his father inside his office and shut the door.

I let out a breath. He definitely was the sexiest man I'd ever laid eyes on. But, despite his six-foot-two stature, obviously fit body, short blond hair that sported a messy textured top like a piece of art, electrifying blue eyes, chiseled cheekbones, and a strong masculine jawline that held the perfect amount of stubble across it, I wasn't interested. And even though he looked like he just stepped right out of a *GQ* magazine, I couldn't be interested. Okay, I lied. I could be if I let myself. He was a freaking Adonis and incredibly sexy, but I hated men at the moment, and I didn't need any distractions in my life, especially when I was starting over and reinventing myself. Plus, he was a playboy, a charmer, a seducer, a one-night kind of man who left a path of shattered hearts and souls wherever he went. That much I could tell.

Chase opened the door and walked out of his father's office, giving me a wink and a smile as he passed by my desk.

"Kinsley, can you come in here, please, and shut the door?" Mr. Calloway asked.

"Yes, Mr. Calloway?"

"Have a seat please." He motioned for me to sit down. "I know my son can come on pretty strong."

"It's fine, Mr. Calloway. I'm not bothered by it."

"Listen, you seem like a really sweet girl and I don't want to see you get hurt. So, it would be in your best interest to not entertain Chase."

"What do you mean?"

"Don't go out with him, and for god sakes, don't sleep with him."

I couldn't help but let out a light laugh.

"I'm assuming he does this thing quite often."

"More than you want to know."

"Thank you for the warning, Mr. Calloway, but you don't have to worry. I'm so anti-men, I didn't even give your son a second look."

"Oh. So, you're a lesbian?"

"No. I'm not a lesbian." I smiled. "Let's just say that I moved here to reinvent myself and to start my life over. I'm not going to let any man distract me from that. I already made that mistake once and it will be a cold day in hell before I let it happen again."

The corners of his mouth curved up in a cunning smile.

"I get the impression you're a very independent and strong woman. Good for you. May I ask why you're working for a temp agency?"

"I just moved here three days ago from Indiana. It was a kind of a spur of the moment move, and the agency called me quickly, so I had to take it for now."

"Well, you have a good head on your shoulders, and I'm lucky the agency sent you over to Calloway Tech."

"Thank you, Mr. Calloway."

"You're welcome, Kinsley. Can you please call the florist and send my fiancée, Penelope, a dozen red roses? We had a little argument this morning." He smirked.

"Of course. I'll do it now." I smiled as I left his office.

Chapter Eight

Kinsley

The work day finally ended, and I hopped into my car, typed the address to the apartment into my phone, and found my way to Santa Monica. As soon as I pulled into a parking space in front of the white buildings, an older woman, whom I presumed was Mrs. Graham, was standing on the sidewalk waiting for me.

"You must be Kinsley." She smiled as she extended her hand.

"And you must be Mrs. Graham." I smiled back as I lightly shook it.

"Follow me, dear, and I'll show you the apartment."

I was a little surprised when I arrived because I was under the impression it was a traditional apartment building. But it wasn't. There were two house-styled buildings that stood next to one another, each building with black wrought iron stairs going up to the second level, and each apartment having their own private entrance. I followed her up the stairs to apartment 2A, where she unlocked the door and invited me to step inside. The living room was quite large with walls that were painted a light gray. Inside the space sat a dark gray sectional with a round glass coffee table in front of it, a matching glass end table on one side, and an entertainment center with a 55-inch television that sat on top. The kitchen was on the smaller side with white cabinets, black granite counter tops, and a small round table that sat four.

"So, Kinsley, where are you living now?" Mrs. Graham asked as we toured the bedroom.

"A motel."

"Oh, dear." She looked at me in confusion.

"I just moved to Los Angeles on Friday. It was an unexpected kind of move. I came out here to start my life over."

"Are you running from someone or something?" she asked.

"Sort of. This has been a dream of mine since I was a kid. I would have been here a couple of years ago, but then I met my ex-boyfriend Henry."

"Ah. So, you pushed it all aside for him." She smiled.

"Pretty much. I went over to his apartment Friday morning to surprise him for his birthday and I found him in bed with my best friend, Krista."

"Oh, dear. I'm so sorry." She placed her hand on my arm.

I had no clue why I told Mrs. Graham something so personal. Maybe it was because she reminded me of Mrs. Buckley and she was very easy to talk to.

"Thank you, but that was the push I needed to finally leave Indiana and move here. I've been saving every dime I've made since I was sixteen years old for this."

"Are you looking for work?"

"I have a job. Today was my first day. I'm a temp for Dean Calloway at Calloway Tech. I'll be working there for at least eight weeks. But I'm still looking for something permanent."

"So what do you think about the apartment?" she asked.

"I love it. I think it's absolutely perfect. How much for the rent?"

"What is your budget?" she asked.

"I really can only afford a thousand dollars a month until I start making more money."

"What a coincidence." She smiled. "That's exactly what the rent is. But you are responsible for all utilities except water."

"Are you serious? There's no way this apartment is a thousand dollars a month."

"It is for you, dear, and if you want it, it's yours."

"Mrs. Graham. I don't know what to say. Thank you so much."

"I'm very selective about whom I rent my apartments to. I've already turned down four people for this place because I felt they weren't the right fit. But you, you're the right fit. My husband passed away a couple of years ago and left me set for the rest of my life. So, I'm not worried about the money. You need a nice place to live and I have one available." She smiled.

"Thank you." I reached over and gave her a hug.

"You're welcome. You can move in tomorrow or even tonight. I'll just need you to sign the lease and the keys are yours. The kitchen is fully stocked with dishes, glasses, silverware, bakeware, and pots and pans. There are some cleaning products under the cabinet, but not many. The bathroom is fully stocked with towels and washcloths, and there are two sets of extra sheets in the linen closet. All you have to do is bring in your clothes." She smiled.

After signing the lease, I drove to the motel, gathered all my things, and checked out. I wasn't spending another night there when I had a beautiful apartment waiting for me. I dragged my suitcase up the steps, into my apartment, and straight to my room, where I began to hang my clothes in the closet. When I was finished, I walked over to the window and stared out at the ocean view from across the street. A sense of peace filled me. My new life had officially started. I had a car, a job, and a home.

I lay in the bubble-filled tub, taking in the relaxing scent of lavender as I unwound from the long day. For some reason, I was thinking about Chase Calloway, so I grabbed my phone and decided to google him.

"L.A.'s sexiest and most eligible bachelor?" I laughed. Of course he was.

I scrolled through the pictures of him at parties and bars surrounded by several women. Women who looked like prostitutes and strippers. Was I surprised? Not at all. Even though today was my first day, I saw the way women looked at him like a dog salivating at a piece of meat. Chase Calloway was simply nothing but a manwhore; a manwhore whom I would keep my distance from.

Chapter Nine

Chase

The doorbell rang, and when I answered it, Lexi was standing there with her head cocked at me.

"Okay, Chase. What is so important that I had to run over here?" she asked as she stepped inside.

"I need to talk to you about something. Can I get you a glass of wine?"

"Sure," she spoke as she set down her purse. "Why couldn't you talk to me about it at the office? Traffic was a bitch getting here."

"I couldn't run the risk of someone overhearing us."

I handed her the glass of wine, grabbed my scotch from the table, and had her follow me out to the patio.

"This sounds serious. Are you in trouble?" she asked with concern.

"No. This is about Kinsley."

"Your dad's temp?" she asked.

"Yes."

"What about her?"

"She seems to not be affected by me." I arched my brow.

Lexi let out a rip-roaring laugh.

"You mean she's not falling to her knees to suck your dick like every other woman in the world?"

"That was uncalled for, Lexi. But yes, something like that. I asked her to go to dinner with me tonight so I could welcome her to Calloway Tech and she declined."

Lexi placed her hand over her heart and widened her eyes.

"Oh my God. Someone actually said no to the great Chase Calloway?"

"I know, right? She said she had plans."

"So what? Maybe she did."

"Lexi." I cocked my head. "Women cancel their plans to go out with me."

"Maybe she's a lesbian." She shrugged.

"That is what I need you to find out." I pointed at her.

"What?" She laughed.

"I need you to befriend her and find out if she's into men or women or both." My brow arched. "If she's bisexual, then I'd still have a chance."

"So, let me get this straight. You want me to become friends with her just so you can find out if she's a lesbian?"

"Yes. As my secretary/personal assistant/sister-like friend,

I've just assigned you a new task."

"Come on, Chase. I'm not going to deceive the smart girl." She smirked. "But I could get to know her as a friend. She seems really nice."

"Excellent. I knew I could count on you." I refilled her glass.

"Did you ever stop to consider that maybe she's just not into you?"

"Impossible." My brows furrowed.

She sighed as she rolled her eyes.

****

The next morning, as I was sitting at my desk, there was a light knock on the door.

"Come in."

When I looked up, I saw Kinsley walk into my office with a file folder in her hand.

"Good morning, Kinsley." I smiled with a hint of excitement.

"Good morning, Chase. Your father asked me to drop this file off to you."

"He did now?" My grin widened as I got up from my chair and took the file from her hand. "Thank you."

"You're welcome," she spoke with an odd look on her face.

"How was your evening?" I asked.

"It was really good. And yours?"

"Not bad. Not at all. So, how about dinner tonight?"

"I don't think so."

"Plans again?" I narrowed my eye at her.

"No." She shook her head. "Just looking forward to a quiet evening alone."

"Oh. I see. Okay, then. Thanks for the file." I held it up.

"You're welcome." She smiled and walked out of my office.

I stood there wondering what the hell was going on. She had to be a lesbian. There could be no other explanation as to why she would turn down dinner with me, twice.

"Lexi," I shouted. "Get in here."

"What's wrong?" She came running into my office.

"Have you found anything out yet about Kinsley Davis?"

She glanced at the watch that was sitting on her wrist.

"Really, Chase?" She cocked her head at me. "It's only nine thirty. She's been here thirty minutes. I haven't had a chance yet."

"Well, chop chop! What are you waiting for? She just turned me down for dinner again."

"I'll go now and ask her if she would like to have lunch together today," she spoke in a calm voice.

"Good idea. As soon as you get back, I want the full report."

She rolled her eyes and walked out of my office.

"Don't roll your eyes at me! This is important!" I shouted before she could close the door.

Chapter Ten

Kinsley

"You're welcome, Mr. Calloway." I smiled as I shut his door.

I had just taken a seat at my desk when a woman walked over to me.

"Hi. I'm Lexi." She smiled. "Welcome to Calloway Tech."

"Thank you. I'm Kinsley."

"I'm sorry I didn't get over here yesterday to introduce myself. It was a crazy busy day," she spoke.

"Oh, that's okay. Please don't give it a second thought."

"Would you like to have lunch together today? There's this great Chinese restaurant just around the corner from here. That is, if you like Chinese food."

"I do, and yes, lunch would be great."

"Perfect. I usually take my lunch at noon. Will that work for you?"

"Noon is good."

"It was nice to meet you, Kinsley." She smiled.

"You too, Lexi."

She seemed really nice, and she was pretty. Five foot four, slender figure, medium-length brown hair with bold blonde highlights, and dark brown eyes. She looked to be about the same age as me or maybe a couple of years older.

Noon rolled around, and I informed Mr. Calloway that I was heading to lunch. When I went back to my desk to grab my purse, Lexi was standing there.

"Ready?" She smiled.

"I am, and I'm starving."

"Me too. Come on."

When we approached the elevator and the doors opened, Chase walked out with a wide grin across his face.

"Well hello, beautiful ladies. Off to lunch?"

I gave him a small smile while Lexi answered him.

"Yes. We'll be back in an hour."

"No need to rush," he spoke. "Take your time and enjoy your food."

We stepped inside the elevator, and as soon as the doors closed, I spoke, "Is he your boss?"

"Unfortunately." Lexi rolled her eyes and I couldn't help but laugh. "Actually, he's really good to work for, sometimes." She smirked. "I've known Chase since I was a kid. His dad and my parents were good friends back when we lived in New York. We stayed in touch all the time when he and his father moved to California, and I would spend the summers here. After I graduated high school, I moved here to attend college, met my fiancé Ben, dropped out of college, and then Chase offered me a job as his secretary/personal assistant."

By time she was finished with her story, we reached the restaurant and took a seat in a booth with high backs.

"Have the two of you ever dated?" I ask and had no clue why.

Lexi laughed. "No. He's like a brother to me."

"You mentioned his dad was friends with your parents. What about his mom?"

"His mom is a whole story on its own. She wasn't around."

"Oh."

"So tell me, why a temp agency? Are you in between jobs or careers?" Lexi asked.

"I just moved here last Friday, and I needed a job ASAP. The agency called, and I took it. It's only temporary until I figure out what I want to do."

"You just moved to California?" she asked. "From where?"

"Berkshire, Indiana."

"I never heard of it."

"I'm not surprised." I smiled. "It's a small town; boring, no excitement whatsoever."

"Do you have family or friends here in California?"

"Nope. I don't know a single person, except for the few people I just met."

"Wow. So you moved here without a plan or a job or anything?"

"Yep. Just me and my suitcase. It was kind of a very sudden move. Like less than a twelve-hour move. I came here to start my life over."

"Let me guess, some douchebag boyfriend broke your heart?"

"Yeah. He was one of the reasons."

We ate our food and Lexi paid the bill.

"How much was mine?" I asked as I pulled out my wallet.

"Put your money away. This lunch is on Chase." She smiled.

When we reached the office, I thanked her again for lunch and went back to my desk. I'd just made a new friend in California.

****

Chase

"Here," Lexi spoke as she threw a receipt at me.

"What's this?" I picked it up.

"That's what you owe me for lunch."

"Why am I paying for your lunch?"

"Because you wanted me to find out information about Kinsley and I did. The least you could do is pay for it."

I sighed as I pulled my wallet from my pocket and handed her some cash.

"Well?" My brow arched.

Lexi shut the door to my office and took a seat.

"She just moved here from Berkshire, Indiana on Friday."

"I knew she wasn't from California!" I pointed at her. "Why did she move?"

"The only thing she said was she moved here to start her life over. I asked her if a douchebag boyfriend broke her heart and she said he was one of the reasons."

"Hmm. So, she's not a lesbian. Damn it! Did she ask about me?" I grinned.

"No."

"Not at all?" I cocked my head in irritation.

"The only thing she asked was if you were my boss."

"That's it? Nothing else?"

"No, Chase. Nothing else. I'm sorry, but I don't think she's interested in you. Especially if she just got her heart broken by some douchebag in Berkshire, Indiana."

"Well, I'm just going to have to fix that for her."

"How? You're the master, the god who breaks women's hearts every day. She's a nice girl and I like her. In fact, I think we could be really good friends. So, I won't let you break her heart."

I narrowed my eyes as I stared at her from behind my desk.

"I wouldn't."

Laughter escaped her. "It's all you know how to do! Leave her alone and move on to the next victim. Oh wait. She did ask if we had ever dated."

"Why would she ask that?"

"Cause I told her I've known you since we were kids."

"Well, if she asked that, then some interest in me must lie somewhere inside her. Why would she care if she wasn't attracted?" I smiled. "You didn't tell her about all the women I date, did you?" My eye narrowed.

"No, and I don't have to. All she has to do is google your name and thousands of images of you and different women pop up. She'd be able to tell right away what a manwhore you are." She smirked.

"That is not true!"

"Sure it is." She laughed. "Google yourself. Are we done here? I have work to do."

"Yes, we're done." I shooed her out of my office.

Picking up my phone, I googled my name and clicked on images.

"Oh shit," I spoke to myself.

Chapter Eleven

Kinsley

The work day was almost over, and I couldn't wait to get home. But first, I had to stop at the grocery store and do some shopping. I was cleaning up my desk when Chase walked over and handed me a flyer.

"What's this?" I asked.

"I'm having a beach party on Saturday with some people here at the office. It would be rude of me not to invite you. It'll be fun. You should come. There will be a lot of alcohol, surfing, sunbathing, volleyball, barbeque, music, and when nightfall hits, a big beautiful bonfire where you can roast marshmallows. I have one every year and it's a blast."

"Thanks. I'll think about it."

"Okay. Have a good night. Still looking forward to spending the evening alone?" He smirked.

"Yes." I grinned.

"Sounds boring, but to each his own. I'll see you tomorrow."

He walked away, and I couldn't help but laugh. I shoved the flyer into my purse and called it a day.

After the market, I took my bags, two at a time, up the stairs and into the kitchen. Once I put away all the groceries, I cooked myself some dinner. Nothing fancy. Just a small homemade pizza and a salad. I took it over to the table and sat down, looking out the window at the palm trees that lightly swayed back and forth. I glanced at my purse, which was sitting on the chair next to me, and pulled out the flyer that Chase had given me. I typed in his address, 2715 Ocean Front Walk, Venice CA, and discovered he only lived fifteen minutes from me. That was a little too close as far as I was concerned. Maybe attending his party would be a good thing. Mrs. Buckley always taught me to look for something positive in a negative. Chase Calloway was a negative, but the positive aspect of his party would be that I would get to know my co-workers and potentially make some new friends. Unlike the backstabbing bitch from back home, the one I grew up with and had known since I was six years old.

As I was cleaning up the kitchen from dinner, there was a knock at the door, and when I opened it, Mrs. Graham was standing there with a plant.

"Mrs. Graham. How are you?"

"Hello, Kinsley, and please call me Delilah."

"Come on in." I smiled.

"This is for you, dear, a little housewarming gift." She handed me the green plant.

"Thank you. That was so sweet. Can I make you a cup of coffee or some tea?"

"A cup of tea would be nice." She smiled as she took a seat at the table. "What's this?" She picked up the flyer.

"Chase Calloway invited me to his beach party on Saturday."

"Oh, that was nice of your boss to do that."

"Not my boss. His son. He works there as well." I grabbed two teabags from the cabinet. "He's actually asked me out to dinner twice."

"And you haven't gone?"

"No." I smiled as I poured hot water in two cups. "He's not my type."

Next thing I knew, Delilah pulled out her phone and brought up a picture of him.

"Oh my. He'd certainly be my type." She winked.

I set the cups on the table and took a seat.

"Are you going to go Saturday?" she asked.

"I don't know. It would be a good opportunity to get to know some people from work."

"And it would be a good opportunity to get out and explore. Now back to Chase Calloway. Why won't you have dinner with him again? And don't tell me he's not your type. This man is everyone's type."

"I'm not looking to go out with any guy right now or for a long time. Remember why I moved here. Plus, he's a total Casanova. You should see how he flirts with all the women. It's like they're under a spell when he's around. It's nauseating." I rolled my eyes.

"Well, I can definitely see why." She smiled. "Just go to the party and have some fun. You deserve it. You're settled here now so there's no reason not to."

"I'll think about it." I smirked.

Chase Calloway

****

The next morning, after Mr. Calloway left for a meeting, I walked over to Lexi's desk.

"Morning, Lexi." I smiled.

"Good morning, Kinsley."

"Are you going to Chase's beach party on Saturday?"

"Yeah. His parties are always the best." She grinned. "I hope you're going to go."

"I don't know. I'm still thinking about it."

"Well, you should. There's going to be a bunch of us there."

"What a way to start the day." Chase smiled as he stopped at Lexi's desk. "Good morning, Kinsley."

"Good morning."

"Did you stop by to see me?" he asked with a smirk on his face.

"No. I came to see Lexi."

Lexi snorted.

"Oh. Well, it's nice to see you're making some friends here. Lexi, I need to go over a few things with you in my office when you're finished."

"I need to get back to my desk anyway," I spoke. "Lunch?" I asked her.

"Sounds good." She smiled.

Chase

"What do you need to go over with me?" Lexi asked as she stepped into my office.

"What did you two talk about?" I responded as I leaned back in my chair.

"Really, Chase?"

"Yes. Get on with it." I waved my hand.

"She asked me if I was going to your party."

"Is she coming?"

"She doesn't know yet."

"Well then, it's up to you to make sure she comes." My brow arched.

"I can't force her to go, Chase."

"True. But you can certainly persuade her, darling. In fact, you can do it at lunch today."

She cocked her head at me. "What is it about her that has you all wound up?"

"I don't know," I spoke with seriousness as I stared at her.

Kinsley Davis was one hell of a sexy woman. I've been with a lot of beautiful women in my life, but there was something different about her that I couldn't quite put my finger on. I wasn't the type of man to really get to know the women I slept with. I honestly could have cared less. I knew they would never amount to anything and that was the way I wanted it, so why bother getting to know them. But, from the moment I saw her, something inside me was pulled towards her. I couldn't explain it even if I tried. Now I was counting on Lexi to make sure Kinsley attended my party. She needed to be there. *I* needed her to be there.

Chapter Twelve

Kinsley

I opened my eyes and let out a big yawn before climbing out of bed and changing into my workout clothes. Over the past week, I made it my daily morning routine to run along the beach before starting my day. Now that I was living in California, I needed to make sure I stayed in shape.

I made a cup of coffee, brushed my teeth, and put my hair up in a ponytail. After placing my Apple watch on my wrist, I grabbed my earbuds and my key, and headed out the door and across the street to the beach, where I would run at least three miles. As I was running and trying to concentrate on the music that was playing in my ears, the only thing I could think about was Chase's party. I knew it would be fun, but at the same time, I was nervous, and I had no idea why.

After my run, I hopped into the shower, put on my bikini, and then slipped into my short sundress. Grabbing my bag, I climbed into my car, punched Chase's address into my phone, and headed to his house. My belly was fluttering with nerves and I had a subconscious suspicion it had something to do with Chase Calloway. His incessant flirting all week was getting to me. Don't get me wrong, he seemed like a nice guy. A guy who was way too sexy to walk the face of the Earth. But again, I knew his type and he wasn't mine. If I was into one-night stands or a casual fling now and again, I'd jump on that in an instant. Would it actually be so bad to try it? After all, I did come to Cali to reinvent myself, try new things and start fresh. I could ditch the old Kinsley Davis and have some fun for once in my life. This was California, not Berkshire, Indiana. Everyone and everything seemed so alive and the vibe was amazing.

I pulled up to the curb down the street from his house since there was nowhere else to park and walked up to the front door, where I rang the doorbell, and a man in a black suit answered.

"Good afternoon, are you here for the Calloway party?" he asked.

"I am." I smiled.

"Please come in. Mr. Calloway is out on the beach with the other guests."

"Thank you."

I stood in the entryway and gasped at his beautiful home. White. Everything was white. From the walls to the furniture and the moldings that were complemented with a white-washed oak floor. As I was following the man in the black suit to the patio door, Lexi came from I wasn't sure where.

"Kinsley!" she exclaimed. "You're here."

"Hi, Lexi." I smiled brightly.

"Come on, let's go down to the beach."

She hooked her arm around mine and led me out the French double doors and to the sand, where people gathered all around, playing volleyball, sunbathing, surfing, and sitting at round tables talking with one another with drinks in their hands.

"Well, hello there, Kinsley." Chase smiled as he scanned me from head to toe. "You look lovely."

"Hi, Chase. Thanks."

"Thanks for coming. You won't be sorry. I'll catch the two of you later. I have to run into the house for something." He smiled.

Lexi walked me over to where she had three chairs set up and a large umbrella staked in the sand to provide some shade.

"Can I get you something to drink? There's every kind of liquor imaginable."

I looked over to my left and saw a bar set up with a bartender shaking cocktails.

"Seriously? He set up a bar out here?" I asked.

"He's Chase Calloway. When he does something, he goes all out. How about a margarita? This guy makes the best watermelon ones."

"That sounds good."

"I'll be right back." She smiled.

"I hope you're having a good time," I heard Chase's voice approach me from behind.

I tilted my head back as he stood over me with a wide grin across his face.

"I've been here five minutes." I smirked.

"Right," he spoke as he set down his surfboard and took a seat in the chair next to me. "Can I get you something to drink?"

"Lexi's getting it for me. Thanks."

"So tell me, Kinsley." He leaned closer to me. "Have you ever been surfing?"

"No. This is actually the first time I've been on a beach. Well, I mean, when I moved here."

"Seriously?" He chuckled. "Why is that and where are you from?"

"I'm from Berkshire, Indiana and that's where I'd been for the past twenty-four years."

"Sounds dreadfully boring."

"Oh. It is. Trust me." I gave him a small smile.

"Here's your margarita," Lexi spoke as she handed it to me. "I'll be right back."

"Welcome to California. May you find the fun you seek." Chase smiled as he held up his glass of scotch to me.

"Thank you." I gave a small smile as I brought my glass to his.

"Surfs up, bro!" Steven yelled as he ran past us with a surfboard.

"I'll catch you later, sweetheart." Chase grinned as he stood up, took off his shirt, grabbed his board, and ran down to the water.

I gulped as I stared at his ripped body. His washboard abs, biceps that were the perfect size, and muscular back made my legs tighten. Lexi made it back and introduced me to a couple of friends of hers. While we all sat and talked, my eyes kept diverting to Chase on his surfboard.

"Let's go swimming!" Lexi spoke with excitement as she stood up and slipped out of her cover-up.

Swimming in the ocean was something I'd always dreamed of, so I took off my sundress and followed Lexi and the other girls out to the water.

Chapter Thirteen

Chase

I was sitting on my surfboard when I saw Kinsley and the girls heading towards the water. Instantly, my cock started to rise as I stared at her in her bikini. Her hourglass figure was something to be desired as well as her perky C-cup breasts, which were scantly covered by her bikini top. The best part about her was that she was natural. Almost all the women I'd been with had breast implants, which I found nothing wrong with, but I preferred natural ones. And from what I could see, they were perfect. Once she was in the water, I paddled my surfboard towards her.

"Get on." I smiled.

"Your surfboard?"

"If you'd prefer to get on something else, I would be more than happy to accommodate you." I smirked.

"I bet you would."

"Come on. Get up here."

She glared at me for a moment and then climbed on my board facing me, and we sat there for a moment while the waves rocked us back and forth.

"What do you think?" I asked.

"It's nice. I take it you surf often?"

"I surf every day. Mostly in the mornings before I head into the office. It helps clear my head."

"I know what you mean. I run every morning before work on the beach across from my apartment."

"I definitely can tell," I spoke.

"Excuse me?" Her brow arched.

"I mean, look at you. You're in great shape. I can tell you take care of yourself. You're sexy." I winked.

"And you're nothing but a big flirt."

"Thank you." I grinned. "It's an art actually."

"And one you've seemed to master very well."

"What can I say? Beautiful women bring out the best in me." I smirked.

"Good to know. Thanks for the chat, but I'm going to head back to shore," she spoke as she tipped off my surfboard and swam away.

I sat there watching her with a narrowed eye. She was a small town girl with no life experience. I could change all that. I could show her what living life in California was all about, and I intended to keep pursuing her until I got what I wanted.

"I saw you chatting Kinsley up," Steven said as he swam up on his board next to me. "Make any progress yet?"

"No. Not yet."

"I'm thinking you need to forget about her. Plus, I don't think she's your type."

"And what is my type?" I glared at him.

"A chick who is kind of dumb. The airhead type. Kinsley isn't that girl. She's smart."

"Exactly, and it's refreshing."

"Ah. I see what's going on here." He pointed at me. "You want her so bad because she turned you down and no chick has ever done that. You see her as a challenge and you won't stop until you've won. She's a game to you."

"Maybe," I spoke as I watched her walk across the sand. "I'm hungry. Shall we eat?" I smiled at Steven.

We paddled our boards back to shore. Once I was out of the water, I tucked my board underneath my arm and set it down by the house.

"Chase!" Amanda yelled as she and her posse came running over.

"Hello there, darling." I grinned as I stared at the four lovely ladies in their bikinis.

"This party is so cool. Thanks for the invite." She threw her arms around me and gave me a hug.

"Well, you're welcome. The party just wouldn't be the same without you beautiful women here."

"Maybe later we could…" She smiled playfully.

"I think that could be arranged. Now if you'll excuse me, I'm going to grab something to eat. Enjoy yourselves and make sure to drink up!" I winked.

I walked over to the buffet table that was set up on my large patio and noticed Kinsley was in line and talking to Jarrod, one of the programmers at the office. He was a good-looking guy and I could see the light in his eyes as he was talking to her. I needed to stop their conversation.

"Hello, Jarrod." I smiled at him as I cocked my head.

"Hey, Chase. Great party."

"Thanks. Kinsley, can I speak with you for a moment," I spoke as I grabbed the plate from her hand.

"Umm. Sure." Her brow furrowed.

I walked her and her plate over to a small table on the patio and set it down.

"What now?" she asked as she took a seat in the chair.

"I just wanted to give you a heads up about Jarrod. He just got out of a three-year relationship."

"Okay? And?"

"I just noticed you getting chummy with him and I thought you should know. He's not in a good place right now."

"I didn't know I couldn't talk to someone who just got out of a relationship. Plus, he seemed fine to me."

"I wasn't saying that. I just saw the way he was looking at you and I thought you should know in case you were thinking about going out with him."

"He didn't ask me out, Chase. We were just having a

conversation. You know, like normal people do? And even if he did ask me out and I went, what business is it of yours?"

"It's totally my business since you refuse to go out with me."

Her eyes narrowed as she brought her fork up to her mouth.

"I won't go out with you because you're a walking STD." She smirked.

"I most certainly am not. I'm totally offended by that comment. I'll have you know that I take protection very seriously. In fact, it's probably the most serious thing I take in life."

"Good to know."

A smile crossed my face. "Now that we've cleared that up, have dinner with me tomorrow night."

"No."

"Come on, Kinsley. You're killing me here. I want to get to know you."

"Why?" She cocked her head.

"To be honest, I don't know. I just do, and you should be flattered because I generally could care less about getting to know someone."

She set down her fork and placed her hand over her heart.

"Mr. Calloway. You're right. I am flattered," she spoke in a sarcastic tone.

I rolled my eyes and sighed.

"Fine. I'm not asking you again. But I will say that you

missed out on one of the best times of your life."

"I'll live." She smiled.

"Enjoy the party, Miss Davis," I spoke as I got up from the table and walked away.

Chapter Fourteen

Kinsley

Rolling my eyes, I finished the amazing food that was on my plate and then mixed and mingled with people from the office. Maybe I was a little harsh by calling him a walking STD. I shouldn't have said that, but he made me mad when he commented about my talking to Jarrod. Who the hell did he think he was? I took in a deep cleansing breath. I wasn't going to let the likes of Chase Calloway affect me anymore.

I was talking to Lexi and Ben, when I looked over and saw Chase surrounded by a group of girls. He was laughing, smiling, and really enjoying himself. The one thing he said that caught my attention was how he could care less about wanting to get to know someone. I wondered why that was.

"Hey, Lexi, can I ask you something about Chase?"

"Sure. What do you want to know?"

"He told me that I should be flattered that he wants to get to know me because he generally could care less about getting to know someone. Why?"

"Well." Her brow arched. "He loves women for what they can give him and what they can give him is sex. That's all he cares about. God, I feel awful for talking about him like that because he truly is an amazing guy and friend. He'd give you the shirt off his back if you needed it. He just doesn't care to get to know the women he sleeps with."

"So you're saying that he pretty much just has meaningless sex with them and that's it?"

"Yes. To Chase, sex is just sex. It has no emotional meaning or attachment."

"When was the last time he was in a relationship?" I asked out of curiosity.

"He's never been in a relationship."

"What?" I laughed. "That's impossible."

"Chase has a lot of issues stemming from his childhood. He doesn't believe in relationships and sometimes he makes it difficult for us who are in them because he loves to voice his opinion."

"I see." I glanced over at him on the sand, still surrounded by women. "I can kind of see his point." I lightly smiled. "After what I witnessed with my ex, it'll be a long time before I trust another man again."

"You never did tell me what happened." She took a sip of her wine.

"We dated for a little over a year. He was the reason why I didn't move out here sooner. I walked in on him and my best friend in bed together."

"Oh. I'm sorry." She placed her hand on my arm.

"Don't be. He told me that it meant nothing and now I realize that it was the best thing that could have happened."

"I can totally understand why you're staying away from guys, and I don't blame you one bit. Trusting someone after that is hard."

"Yeah, it is." I gave her a small smile. "And I'll never make the mistake of putting my life on hold for someone else."

****

The sun was starting to set, and it was such an amazing sight. I saw Chase standing by the water alone, gazing out the sunset, so I decided to walk over to him.

"It's beautiful," I spoke.

"It sure is. This is something I will never get tired of seeing."

I glanced over at him as he stood there with his hands tucked into the pockets of his shorts.

"Chase, I'm sorry for calling you a walking STD. I didn't mean it."

"Nah. It's fine. You don't have to apologize."

"I do, and again, I'm sorry."

"Apology accepted." He smiled as he looked over at me. "Are you liking it in California so far?"

"Actually, I'm loving it." I grinned.

"Chase! We need one more person on our team for volleyball. Come play with us!" a girl in a teeny-weeny bikini shouted.

"I'll be right there, darling," he shouted back. "They need

me."

"Then you better not disappoint them."

"Do you want to play? I'm sure we could squeeze you in."

"Nah." I waved my hand. "You go ahead."

"Okay. We'll talk later?"

"Yeah. Later." I smiled.

He walked away, and I stared into the vast open water. I couldn't stop thinking about what Lexi said and how Chase had many issues stemming from his childhood. Who didn't? I remembered her telling me when we first met that his mother was a whole other story and she wasn't around when he was a child. If anyone could relate, it would be me. But somehow, I didn't think I was as fucked up as he was. All this thinking was bringing back the memories I buried so long ago. Memories I wanted to pretend never existed. I needed a drink, so I walked over to the bar and ordered a shot of tequila, downed it, and ordered another one.

"Look at you, Kinsley Davis." Chase smiled as he walked over to the bar. "I didn't think small town girls did shots."

"This one does." I pointed to myself.

"Well, good for you, letting your wild side out. I'll have what she's having." He grinned at the bartender.

Chase and I stood there, doing shot after shot. Soon others joined us. I was having the time of my life. Laughing, dancing, and having ridiculous conversations. For the first time in my life, I let loose, lived in the present moment, and did what I wanted to do without having to worry about anyone else.

Chapter Fifteen

Kinsley

A noise woke me from a deep sleep. I opened my eyes and placed my hand on my forehead, somehow thinking that it would stop it from pounding. I looked around my bedroom in confusion, for I didn't remember coming home last night. I started to panic at the thought that I drove home and I could have killed someone in the drunken state that I was in.

"Ah. You're awake." Chase smiled as he entered my bedroom.

"What are you doing here?" I asked as I pulled the sheet up to my neck.

"I brought you home last night. Don't you remember?"

"No. I don't remember anything."

"Of course you don't. You were too drunk. Good job, by the way." He grinned.

"For what?"

"For letting your party girl out. Stay right where you are. I'll be right back."

I was confused, and as hard as I tried, the last thing I

remembered was doing shots at the bar. A few moments later, Chase walked into the bedroom with a cup of coffee.

"Drink up."

"You drove me home?" I asked as I took the cup from him.

"Yes, and you're welcome."

"How? You drank just as much as I did."

"Alcohol and I have an understanding. We're like best friends." He smirked.

"How did you know where I lived?"

"I wish I could say I got your address from your driver's license, but you don't have a California license yet. Which, by the way, you better do quickly. So I checked your google maps on your phone."

"Thank you. I appreciate it, but why are you still here?"

"By time I got you in your apartment, held your hair while you vomited in the toilet, and then put you to bed, I was too tired to drive home, so I just passed out on your couch."

"Thank you for bringing me home." I sipped my coffee as I still had a tight grip on the sheet.

"You're welcome."

"What about my car?"

"I had one of the guys, who was a designated driver, follow me here with it. Your keys are on the kitchen table."

"There isn't anything else I should know about, is there?"

"Like what? Oh right. You're asking if we had sex, aren't you?" He grinned.

I gulped as I slowly nodded my head.

"No. We didn't. I'd prefer you to be sober when we do."

"We aren't ever having sex."

"Never say never, darling." He winked. "Anyway, I have to go. If you need anything, I've programmed my cell into your phone. Have a good day, Kinsley. By the way, you don't have any contacts in your phone but three people. I found that a little strange."

"You went through my phone?"

"No. I noticed it when I put my number in. Who's Reece?"

"My cab driver," I replied with furrowed brows.

"You are a strange girl, Miss Davis." He smiled as he walked out of my bedroom and out the door.

I set my coffee cup on the nightstand and pulled the sheet over my head as I sank down into the depths of my comfortable bed. I was hungover, and I hated myself for drinking as much as I did. Chase was right; I let my party girl out, and today I was regretting it. After taking quite a long nap, I showered and changed into a pair of fresh pajamas. I hadn't eaten all day thanks to my queasy stomach, but now that it was seven o'clock, I was hungry. As I was rummaging through the refrigerator, trying to figure out what to make for dinner, there was a knock at my door. It was probably Delilah stopping by to see how the party was yesterday.

"Chase," I spoke in shock when I opened the door. "What

are you doing here?"

"I figured since you won't go out to dinner with me, I'd bring dinner to you." He smiled as he held up two large plastic bags. "Plus, I was in your refrigerator this morning and I noticed you didn't have any food. You really need to go shopping. May I come in?"

"Yeah. Sure. You didn't have to bring me dinner."

"I know I didn't, but I figured you hadn't eaten all day because of your hangover." He took the bags into the kitchen and set them on the counter. "I brought a variety of food since I wasn't really sure what you liked. We have two different kinds of salads, grilled chicken, salmon, seasoned rice, mashed potatoes, sweet potatoes, green beans, and asparagus. Oh, and a pasta dish."

"Did you order the whole menu?" I laughed.

"Almost." He smirked.

I grabbed a couple of plates and some silverware and took them over to the table while Chase set all the food down.

"I don't suppose you want any alcohol, do you?" He smirked as he held up a bottle of scotch.

Just looking at the bottle made my stomach churn.

"No. I'll stick with water."

I grabbed a bottle of water from the fridge and we both sat down at the table.

"This all looks and smells really good, but if you're expecting to get sex out of it, you can forget it." I smirked.

"Kinsley, darling, I didn't bring you dinner expecting to get sex. Actually, I had plans tonight, but they got cancelled, and believe it or not, I had nothing else to do. Plus, I knew you wouldn't have plans."

"Excuse me?" My brow arched. "Are you insinuating that I don't do anything or go anywhere?"

"Yes." He smiled. But I knew with what you drank last night, you'd be hungover all day. So, tell me about Kinsley Davis."

"What do you want to know?" I asked.

"Everything." He grinned. "But seriously, why did you move to California?"

"It's always been a dream of mine to get out of that small town and away from everyone in it."

"Even your parents?" He cocked his head.

"My dad died when I was six, and yes, even my mom."

"Well, I can't imagine your mom being too happy that you moved across the country. Did she try and stop you or try to talk you out of it?"

"I didn't talk to her about it. I left a note."

His brow arched as he took a sip of his scotch, and instantly, I noticed a look of disapproval cross his face.

"I see. Don't you think that was a little harsh and unfair?"

"No." I narrowed my eye at him.

"So you think running away has no effect on anybody who cares about you?" he spoke in a stern voice.

"Excuse me?"

"Don't you think leaving a note was the coward's way out?" his stern voice spoke. "Is that what you normally do? Leave a note and run?"

"Who the fuck do you think you are?" I shouted at him. "You know nothing about me or the way I grew up."

"You're right, I don't. But I don't think anyone deserves that kind of disrespect, no matter what."

I could feel my blood pressure rise as my skin felt like it had been set on fire.

"Thank you for dinner, Mr. Calloway. I think it's time you left," I spoke in a stern voice as I got up from my chair and took my plate over to the sink.

"I think that's a good idea," he spoke as he walked out of my apartment, shutting the door behind him.

I stood at the sink, my fingers tightly gripping the edge of the counter as I tried to process what had just happened.

Chapter Sixteen

Chase

I climbed into my car and began to drive home with the music blaring as loud as it could go. My fingers gripped the steering wheel as I tried to calm down. Kinsley Davis was a trigger and I sure as hell didn't see that coming. I changed my mind about home and kept driving to a club I visited on a regular basis called Phantom.

I pulled up to the valet and tossed my keys to Kevin.

"Good evening, Mr. Calloway." He smiled.

"I wouldn't really say there's anything good about it. At least not yet." I winked.

I walked through the doors and headed straight to the bar.

"Hello there, Chase." Linda seductively smiled as she pulled a glass down and poured me a scotch.

"Hey, Linda."

"What's wrong?"

"Nothing. Just a bad night." I threw back my drink and set down my glass in front of her.

"Why don't you tell me all about it?" she spoke as she leaned across the counter and ran her finger up my arm.

"I don't feel like talking about it."

"Okay. If you do, you know where to find me." She smiled.

I threw back my second drink and stared at the beautiful women that were in my sight, especially the tall brunette with the bright red lipstick that was headed my way.

"Hello there, handsome." She smiled.

"Well hello, gorgeous. May I buy you a drink?"

"Of course." She took the seat next to mine.

****

"Hello, beautiful." I answered with a smile.

"Are you coming into the office today or do I just have to sit around and play the guessing game?" Lexi asked.

"I'm on my way in now. I'm about fifteen minutes out."

"Okay. I'll let Steven know. The two of you had a meeting scheduled twenty minutes ago."

"I know. Tell him I'm on my way."

I was in a fantastic mood today and nothing was going to ruin it, except maybe the backup that I suddenly found myself in.

"Good morning, love." I smiled at Lexi. "Can you let Steven know I'm here?"

"Sure." She gave me an odd look.

Chase Calloway

I walked into my office, set my briefcase next to my desk, and took a seat.

"Here's your coffee. Steven's on a call. He said give him about ten minutes." She cocked her head at me and narrowed her eye. "Rough night last night?"

"Actually," I grinned, "Alania was a bit rough."

"I can tell by the hickey on your neck. How old was she? Seventeen?" Her brow arched.

"Don't be ridiculous, Lexi. Is it that bad?"

"It's visible and ridiculous for someone your age. What's going on with you and Kinsley?"

"What do you mean?" I sipped my coffee.

"You drove her home after the party. Anything happen?"

"No. You know I don't take advantage of drunk women unless I'm totally plastered myself. Anyway, I don't want to talk about her. No, wait. Actually, I do. Did you know that when she left Indiana, she wrote her mom a note and left without even talking to her or saying goodbye?"

"No. I didn't know that. When did she tell you?"

"Last night."

"I thought you were with the seventeen-year-old last night." She smirked.

I rolled my eyes.

"I took dinner over to her place. I figured since she refused to go out to dinner with me, I'd bring dinner to her."

"Then how did you end up with the seventeen-year-old and the hickey?"

"For fucks sake, will you stop saying that! I may or may not have gotten a little angry and she asked me to leave."

"What did you do to her?!" Lexi's voice raised as her eyes glared at me.

"All I said was that leaving a note was the coward's way out and it was disrespectful. Then I asked her if she made a habit of leaving notes and running."

She placed her hand over her eyes and slowly shook her head.

"It was a trigger response, Lexi."

"You don't know her circumstances, Chase."

"It doesn't matter." I leaned back in my chair.

There was a knock on the door and Steven walked in.

"Hey, I just saw Kinsley out there and she said if I saw you to tell you that your dad wants to see you in his office."

"Shit." I sighed. "I'll come down to your office for our meeting after I see him."

"Sure, bro. Hey," he smiled, "nice hickey."

"She was seventeen." Lexi smirked at him.

"Dude! Shut the fuck up! Awesome!" Steven replied.

"She was not, and if you say that again," I pointed at her, "I'm firing you!"

Lexi sat there with a smile on her face as I walked out of my office and down to my dad's. The last thing I wanted to do was run into Kinsley today, but it couldn't be helped since she was sitting right outside his office.

"He wanted to see me?" I asked as I stared at her.

She wouldn't look at me and kept typing away on the computer.

"Yes. But he's on a phone call right now," she spoke in a flat tone.

I lightly tapped on his door and slowly opened it. When he saw me, he waved me in and motioned for me to sit down. His call only lasted a few moments, and when he hung up, he glared at my neck.

"Really, son?" He sighed. "At least cover the damn thing up." He shook his head. "K-Com is highly impressed with your program and they're going to go with it. Good job, son."

"Thanks, Dad." I smiled.

"Listen, Chase. You're thirty years old. Have you considered that maybe it's time to find a nice girl and settle down?"

I couldn't help but laugh. "Me, settle down? Right. Never happening, Dad."

"This party life of yours can't go on forever."

"Why not?"

"Because, son, it's not the way to live."

"But marrying and divorcing four times is?" I arched my brow at him. "And now you're marrying bridezilla for the fifth time? You do know she's only after your money, right?"

"I made her sign a prenuptial agreement and it's ironclad. If she was only in it for the money, she wouldn't have signed it and called off the wedding. But she didn't. She was more than happy to sign it. You never gave her a chance, Chase. You hated her right off the bat, and I don't understand why. I love her."

"Just like you loved Mom?" I arched my brow.

"I loved your mother." He pointed his finger at me. "And I'm not discussing this anymore. Get your fucking life together and act like a Calloway or there will be consequences."

"Consequences?" I cocked my head. "If it weren't for me, Calloway Tech wouldn't be where it's at today; a company worth twenty-billion-dollars. Don't you forget that!" I spoke through gritted teeth as I got up from my seat and flew out the door back to my office.

Chapter Seventeen

Kinsley

I could hear parts of the heated argument between Chase and his father. I was still angry with him for what he said to me last night, and the instant change I saw in him was unreal. It was like he was a totally different person. If I didn't need this damn job so bad, I would quit so I didn't have to see him again. The night of the party, I felt something. I didn't want to, and I tried to ignore it, but I couldn't. Then when I woke up and he was there, in my apartment, I felt it again. He hurt me with his words, especially calling me a coward. He hadn't a clue, and the more I thought about it, the angrier I became.

It was the end of the work day and everyone had left. I stayed behind to finish typing up a proposal Mr. Calloway gave me at the last minute. When I was finished, I set it on his desk, grabbed my purse, and headed to the parking garage for my car. Once I climbed inside and turned the key, the car wouldn't start.

"Oh, come on. Don't do this to me," I spoke in frustration.

I popped the hood, got out of the car, and looked underneath it.

"What are you doing?" Chase asked as he pulled up.

"My car won't start."

He shut off his car, got out, and stood next to me.

"What exactly are you looking for?" he asked.

"I think it's the starter that's bad. I'm just checking for any loose connections."

"And you know a thing or two about cars?"

"Yes. A little bit. Don't you?" I glanced over at him.

"No. I know nothing about them."

"I'm not surprised."

"What's that supposed to mean?" he asked.

"Nothing. Just go. I'm going to have to call a tow truck," I spoke with irritation as I pulled my phone from my purse.

"I know a guy. Let me make a call, and then I'll drive you home."

"I can call an Uber."

"You're not calling an Uber." He sighed.

"I'm sure you have plans tonight." I stared at the hickey on his neck. "Maybe round two from last night."

"Don't worry about my plans. I'm not leaving you here alone."

He walked away and made a call. A few moments later, he walked over to me.

"Carl is on his way. He'll be here in about twenty minutes and tow it to his shop, which isn't too far from here."

"Thanks." I looked down.

"Why are you here this late anyway?" he asked.

"Your dad gave me a proposal at the last minute and it needed to be typed up for his meeting tomorrow morning."

"Sounds like him." He rolled his eyes.

We both leaned up against my car, me looking down at the ground and him standing there with his hands tucked into the pockets of his dress pants. It was awkward to say the least, yet somehow, I felt the strong need to tell him about Henry.

"Me and Henry were together for a little over a year. It was his birthday and I wanted to surprise him. So, I took the day off work, stopped at his favorite bakery in the morning, went to his apartment, and found him in bed with my best friend, Krista. They claimed they only slept together twice, but I knew it was more than that."

"I'm sorry," Chase softly spoke. "That must have been quite a shock."

"I left his apartment, went home, packed what I could, and hopped on a plane here. I only stayed in Indiana because of him. A year of my life wasted when I could have already been here and established."

The tow truck pulled up and I told Carl that it was most likely the starter. He looked at me with a smile and spoke, "A girl who knows about cars. I like that." He hooked my car up and drove away.

"Climb in," Chase spoke as he opened the passenger door for me.

"Thanks."

He sped out of the parking garage and I held on for dear life. But watching him drive his sports car was quite a turn on. Something I needed to get out of my head.

"This isn't the way to my apartment," I spoke.

"I know. We're making a stop first." He glanced over at me.

"Where?"

"You'll see." He smirked.

He pulled into the parking lot of a restaurant called Water Grill Downtown.

"Why are we here?" I asked.

"I'm starving and I'm sure you are too. So, before I take you home, we're going to eat."

He got out of the car and opened my door.

"You don't have to open the door for me," I spoke with irritation as I climbed out. The last thing I wanted to do was have dinner with him.

"I *am* a gentleman."

"No you're not." I rolled my eyes as I walked ahead of him.

"How dare you," he spoke.

Once we entered the restaurant that had a two-hour wait, we were seated immediately because L.A.'s sexiest and most eligible bachelor had arrived.

"Impressed?" He smirked.

"Not really." I picked up my menu.

I heard the sharp intake of his breath as I held the menu up to my face.

"Chase Calloway." A pretty blonde-haired waitress smiled.

"Kara, darling. How are you?"

"I'm good. It's been a while." She winked.

I sat there with a narrowed eye as I watched the nauseating interaction between the two of them.

"It has. Maybe we should catch up over a drink sometime." Chase grinned.

"I'd love that. Call me." She stood there swooning over him as she bit down on her bottom lip.

"Excuse me," I spoke. "I totally hate to interrupt this special moment between the two of you, but can we order?"

"Oh sure." She turned to me, holding her notepad in her hand. "What can I get you, sweetie?"

"I'll have the sea scallops and the butternut squash," I replied.

"And for you, handsome?" She turned to Chase.

"I'll have the Chilean sea bass and mashed potatoes. Also bring us a bottle of Prosecco."

"You got it." She grinned as she took our menus and walked away.

I was blown away by his behavior with other women when he was with a woman. Not only was it rude but insulting as well.

"Why did you tell me about your ex earlier?" he asked.

"I don't know. You wanted to know why I left California in such a hurry."

"Was he the only reason? Because I find it a little strange that you'd just skip town and move to a place where you don't know anyone at all or have a place to live or a job over a guy. I kind of find that being a little unstable."

"He was the only reason why I stayed. And aren't you the pot calling the kettle black."

Kara, our waitress, brought the bottle of Prosecco and poured some into each of our glasses.

"Thank you, darling." Chase winked, and I wanted to vomit. "What do you mean by that?" he asked as he narrowed his eye at me.

"You've slept with just about every woman in Los Angeles and god knows where else. Talk about being unstable."

"No, sweetheart. That's not being unstable. I happen to enjoy sex with beautiful women. There's nothing wrong with that. It's called life. Maybe you should try it sometime."

"You're right, Chase. It's not about being unstable. It's about being insecure." I cocked my head.

He let out a chuckle. "Me," he pointed to himself, "insecure? You're delusional, darling. I'm the most secure person there is."

"Keep telling yourself that. Because deep down, you use sex as a coping mechanism."

"Okay. First of all, we're not talking about me. We're talking about you. I asked you the question, remember? Plus, you don't know a damn thing about me to be making judgments like that." He threw back his drink.

"And you don't know a damn thing about me either," I growled.

Chapter Eighteen

Chase

This woman was fucking unbearable. How dare she say those things to me. I helped her with her car, treated her to a nice dinner, and that was how she behaved? This was totally unacceptable.

"Enjoy your dinner." Kara smiled as she set our plates down in front of us.

"I'll try," I spoke as I glared at Kinsley.

I never had to deal with a woman this difficult before, and no woman had ever talked to me the way she had. She might have been beautiful, but she was stubborn, intense, and a smart mouth. I guessed that was how small town girls were raised, and I didn't like it one bit.

We ate our dinner in silence, neither one of us saying a word. She owed me an apology and I wanted it.

"You owe me an apology," I spoke.

"Excuse me? *I* owe you an apology?" She pointed to herself. "No, jerk! You owe me an apology."

I was taken aback by her calling me a jerk.

"I don't owe you shit. I was nice enough to help you out with your car and treat you to this nice dinner and that's how you treat me?"

She let out a roaring laugh. A laugh so loud that the people at the table next to us looked over.

"In two days, you have called me a coward, disrespectful, and unstable!"

"Oh no he didn't," the lady at the table next to us looked at Kinsley and spoke.

"Oh, but he did." She slowly nodded her head.

"Shame on you!" The lady waved her finger at me. "If you were my son, you'd get a good whooping."

"Well then, thank god I'm not," I mumbled. "Okay. Everyone needs to calm down. Kinsley, I'm sorry for calling you those things."

"No you're not." She pursed her lips.

I sighed. "Can we please just finish our dinner so I can take you home?"

"Fine," she spoke.

Suddenly, I looked up and saw my father and Penelope following the hostess to a table. Shit. If he saw me with Kinsley, he wasn't going to be happy. I gulped as he saw me and walked over to our table.

"Chase, Kinsley," he spoke with a disapproving tone and then turned to me with a glaring eye.

"Hi, Mr. Calloway." Kinsley smiled.

"Hey, Dad."

"So the two of you are having dinner together?" he asked with suspicion.

"When I was leaving the office, I saw Kinsley in the parking garage and her car wouldn't start. So, I called a tow truck and offered to drive her home and we stopped here to get something to eat on the way."

"I see. Kinsley, this is my fiancée Penelope. Penelope, this is my temporary secretary, Kinsley Davis."

"Nice to meet you." She smiled as she extended her hand.

"It's nice to meet you too," Kinsley spoke as she placed her hand in Penelope's.

"Well, then, we'll let you two finish your dinner. I'll see you both tomorrow morning."

"See ya, Dad."

We finished our dinner and I waved Kara over for the check.

"Don't forget about that drink, Chase." She winked.

"I won't, darling."

Kinsley reached into her purse, grabbed some cash, and threw it on the table.

"What's that for?" I asked.

"My half of dinner."

"Don't be ridiculous. I'm paying," I spoke as I picked up the cash and tried to hand it back to her.

"I didn't ask you to take me to dinner. Plus, I don't want you holding it over my head." Her brow arched.

"Kinsley, come on. Please." I cocked my head with a small smile.

"Fine." She grabbed the cash from my hands and got up from her seat.

"Don't I even get a thank you?" I held out my hands.

She ignored me and walked out the door. As soon as I dropped her off at her apartment and she walked away without as so much as a goodbye, I went home and poured myself a drink. Kinsley Davis was an insufferable woman and she drove me insane. I'd never felt this kind of contempt before with any woman and it bothered me. Why was I letting her get under my skin?

The next morning, I woke up in a bad mood. I didn't sleep well, and I tossed and turned all night.

"Good morning, Chase." Lexi smiled brightly.

I glanced at her and walked into my office, throwing my briefcase on the couch. Suddenly, I heard the door shut.

"Okay, what's going on? Who has your panties in a twist?" Lexi asked as she handed me a cup of coffee.

"Nothing is going on, and no one, as you so eloquently put it, has my panties in a twist."

"I call bullshit. I've known you forever, Chase."

Suddenly, the door opened, and Steven walked in.

"Not now, Steven," I spoke as I took a seat in my chair.

"What's going on?" he asked.

"Someone has Chase's panties in a bunch and he won't tell me who or what happened to put him in such a foul mood this morning."

"Oh. Is that so? Do tell." He smiled as he took a seat across from my desk.

I sighed as I leaned back in my chair and looked up at the ceiling.

"It's Kinsley."

"Now what happened?" Lexi asked in a monotone voice.

"When I was leaving last night, I saw her in the parking garage and her car wouldn't start. I called a tow truck and on the way home, we stopped and grabbed some dinner."

"Let me guess." Steven grinned. "She refused to have sex with you."

I rolled my eyes and shook my head. "No. Sex wasn't even on the table. She told me about her catching her ex and her best friend in bed and that's why she moved here so suddenly. I asked her if that was the only reason because it seemed a little unstable."

"Oh, Chase. You didn't."

"You called her unstable?" Steven asked.

"She told me that the only reason I have sex with so many women is because I'm insecure."

Lexi snorted, and I shot her a dirty look.

"When I debated with her about it, she told me I use sex as a coping mechanism."

Lexi snorted again, and I pointed my finger at her.

"Then I told her she owed me an apology and she voiced rather loudly that I owed her one, and she refused to apologize."

"The two of you need to have sex and get it over with," Steven spoke.

"I've never seen you like this before," Lexi said. "Kinsley is a strong and independent woman. You're not used to that. All the women you sleep with are airheads."

"That is not true," I spoke.

"Yeah, bro. It is," Steven agreed. "You don't let women get to you at all, so us having this conversation tells me that you're afraid of her."

"Don't be ridiculous." I chuckled. "Why the fuck would I be afraid of Kinsley?"

"Because you don't know what to do with her," Lexi replied. "You're not used to this kind of challenge. You snap your fingers and women drop to their knees for you. But with Kinsley, you snap your fingers and she runs the other way."

"She does not, Lexi. Maybe she doesn't know what to do with me. After all, she's from a small town with probably no experience at all. Maybe that's why her boyfriend cheated on her."

"That's low, Chase. Even for you." Lexi's brows furrowed.

"Yeah. Perhaps it was. I need to get to work and so do the

both of you." I pointed at them.

Chapter Nineteen

Kinsley

Instead of running my usual three miles a day, I ran six. I was up all night, tossing and turning because of that insufferable man named Chase Calloway. I was running from the thoughts in my head about him. Sure, he was sexy, gorgeous, and hot, but he was an asshole who thought he could talk to women any way he wanted to. Maybe he could get away with it with the brainless, low self-esteemed women he fucked on a daily basis, but not with me. Why was it that when I decided to stay away from him, we kept crossing paths?

I was sitting at my desk when Mr. Calloway walked past.

"Good morning, Kinsley. Can I see you in my office for a second?"

"Sure, Mr. Calloway."

I got up from my seat and followed him into his office.

"How was your dinner last night?" he asked.

"It was fine."

"And Chase made sure you got home safely?"

"Yes." I gave him an odd look.

"And everything's okay?"

"Yes, Mr. Calloway."

"Okay then. You may go." He nodded.

I got up from my seat with confusion, and as I headed towards the door, something inside me snapped.

"No!" I abruptly turned around and faced him. "Things are not okay. Your son is an insufferable man. He's rude, arrogant, thinks he knows everything, and he's cocky."

"I won't disagree." He smirked. "I take it you and Chase aren't getting along?"

"Getting along? I can't even stand to be in the same room with him."

"Kinsley, I'm sorry, but I have to ask. Did you two sleep together?"

"No! Of course not."

He sat behind his desk with a confused look on his face.

"If you didn't sleep together, then where is all this coming from?"

"What do you mean?"

"Usually this type of behavior and animosity comes after the sex with Chase."

"I did not sleep with your son, Mr. Calloway. He's just a judgmental asshat."

"I like that." He laughed as he pointed to me. "Asshat."

"He told me that I was unstable, so I told him that he was insecure and that's why he sleeps around with anyone that has a vagina. I told him he uses sex as a coping mechanism."

"And what did he say to that?"

"He wasn't happy about it and reverted the conversation back to me being unstable."

"You're far from unstable, Kinsley. Don't let my son's words upset you."

"Trust me, I'm not, and I'm sorry for the rant. It just came out."

"It's fine, dear. Don't give it another thought. I'm always here to listen if you need an ear."

"Thanks, Mr. Calloway." I gave him a small smile as I walked out of his office.

****

Chase

I'd just gotten back from lunch when my father walked into my office and shut the door. I'd been waiting for this all day.

"I'm surprised it took you this long to talk to me," I spoke.

"About what?" he asked as he took a seat across from my desk.

"About me and Kinsley at dinner last night."

"Ah, that. Well, you had a reasonable excuse. That was nice of you to help her out with her car. I'm sure she appreciated it."

"Appreciated it?" I cocked my head. "She didn't appreciate anything. That woman is insufferable, Dad."

"I see," he spoke as he stroked his chin. "Why do you say that?"

"She told me I was insecure and that's why I sleep around. Like what the hell does she mean by that? She has a smart mouth, that one." I pointed at him. "Maybe you should call the temp agency and get someone else. I'm surprised you put up with that, Dad."

"She's a good temp and I like her a lot. She isn't going anywhere. In fact, as soon as Audrey comes back to work, I may find Kinsley a permanent position here at Calloway Tech." He smiled.

"We don't have any openings." I narrowed my eye at him.

"It's my company. I'll create a position if I have to."

I took in a deep breath. "It's half my company too."

"But I have the majority rule. I have a meeting to get to." He looked at his watch. "Oh, by the way, I'm having a little get together at the house this Saturday and you'll be there. Understand?"

"What if I already have plans?"

"Cancel them. Family is more important," he spoke as he walked out of my office.

I managed not see Kinsley today, which was a good thing because I needed to stop thinking about her and her smart mouth. I finished my work for the day and was in desperate need of a drink and some fun. I needed to go home and change because I was meeting Steven and Alex at Phantom tonight for a guy's night out. I shut down my computer, grabbed my briefcase, and headed to the parking garage, where I saw Kinsley getting into Lexi's car. I don't know why I did it, but I pulled my phone from my pocket and dialed Carl.

"Hey, Chase, what's up?"

"Hi, Carl. Do you know when Kinsley's car is going to be ready?"

"Tomorrow afternoon, it'll be done."

"Okay. Thanks."

"No problem, Chase. Take care."

"You too."

I was at the club with Steven and Alex, drinking and deciding which beautiful woman I was going to be spending the night with.

"Your days of doing this are going to be coming to an end," I spoke to Alex.

"Yeah, man, once you're married, you're done for," Steven spoke.

"Nah. Things will change a little bit, but we'll always have guy night. I'm not giving that up," Alex said.

"And what about when the babies come?" Steven asked. "You're going to be expected to stay home every single night."

"I'm never having kids." I smiled. "Too much work and too much of a lifestyle change."

"Yeah. God forbid you think of someone other than yourself." Alex grinned.

"Damn right! I love my life too much to ever be burdened with a kid and a girlfriend or wife." I held up my drink.

"Well, we're having kids. We agreed on two," Alex spoke. "I can't wait to be a dad."

"Good for you, Alex," I spoke as I placed my hand on his shoulder. "Fatherhood isn't for everyone."

I couldn't stop thinking about Kinsley. Damn it. I pulled my phone from my pocket and decided to send her a text message. Why? I had no clue.

"Hey, I know your car is in the shop still, so I can pick you up tomorrow morning for work."

Twenty minutes went by and still no response from her. It was nine o'clock and she was probably sleeping since she had no life.

"Hey, Chase?" Alex tapped me on the shoulder. "Isn't that Kinsley out there on the dance floor?"

"What? Where?"

"Right over there." He pointed. "In the short black dress dancing with that good-looking guy." He smirked.

"I'll be damned. It is her."

Chapter Twenty

Chase

I stood there and watched her as she danced in her tiny black dress and stiletto heels. She was sexy as fuck and my cock was starting to get hard. But who the hell was she here with and who the fuck was that guy with his hands on her ass? I scurried over to the dance floor and lightly grabbed hold of her arm with a smile.

"Hello, love. Can I have a word with you?"

"Chase. What the hell are you doing here?" she shouted over the blaring music.

"Excuse us for a moment," I spoke to the douche-looking guy she was dancing with.

I pulled her over to the corner, where we could attempt to have a conversation.

"What are you doing?" she asked through gritted teeth.

"I should be asking you the same thing, but I see you're letting your party girl out again."

"So what? It's none of your business."

"But it is when you're dancing with some douchebag-looking guy and he has his hands all over your ass. You're my father's secretary, and somehow, I feel it's my duty to make sure you're safe from the could-be rapists, murderers, and kidnappers here in Los Angeles. If something happened to you and I was there, my father would blame me."

"Oh my God, will you just shut up!"

"Seriously, though, who are you here with?"

"Lexi. I'm here with Lexi. She's in the bathroom."

"Oh. Well, I sent you a text message earlier and you didn't respond."

"I haven't checked my phone. Why did you text me?"

"I can pick you up for work in the morning since your car is still in the shop," I spoke.

"No," she deadpanned.

"No?" I arched my brow. "How are you getting there?"

"I'll Uber it."

"Don't be ridiculous. That costs money. You can ride in with me for free. So put your stubbornness aside because I'm picking you up in the morning."

"There you are. Hey, Chase." Lexi smiled as she walked over to us. "What are you doing here?"

"Same thing you are. Having a good time." I grinned.

"Everything okay?" She looked at Kinsley.

"Of course everything's okay. I was just telling Kinsley that I'll pick her up in the morning at eight o'clock for work since her car is still in the shop. Right, Kinsley?"

"Fine." She rolled her eyes.

"Hey, Kinsley, want to finish our dance?" The douche-looking guy walked over.

"She's done dancing with you. Move along." I waved my hand.

"And who the fuck are you?" He got in my face.

"The guy who's going to give you ten seconds to step away before I punch you in the face."

He put his hands up and took a few steps back, then suddenly lunged at me, hitting me in the eye.

"Shit."

I raised my fist and punched him square in the jaw, sending him to the ground. Before he had a chance to get up, security came and threw him out of the club.

"Are you okay?" Kinsley asked as she looked at my eye, which was starting to swell.

"Oh. That's going to look nasty in the morning," Lexi spoke.

Steven and Alex ran over to where we were standing.

"A little late, guys." I looked at them.

"Looks like you handled it on your own." Steven laughed.

"You really should get some ice on that," Kinsley spoke.

"I'll be fine."

"I called Ben and he's waiting outside for us," Lexi spoke to Kinsley.

"I'll drive her home. She's on my way. It's out of the way for you and I'm leaving now anyway."

"Are you sure?" Lexi's eye narrowed at me.

"Yeah. If it's okay with Kinsley."

"It's fine, and he's right, I'm on his way home," she spoke to Lexi.

After we said our goodbyes to Lexi, Steven, and Alex, we left the club and got into my car. My eye was throbbing, and my knuckles were swelling.

"You didn't have to tell him to move along," Kinsley spoke.

"Yes, I did. He looked shady."

She let out a laugh, which made me smile. I pulled up to her apartment building and she told me to come inside.

"You need to get ice on that hand and eye. Come up and let me help you."

"I'm fine, Kinsley. I'll do it when I get home."

"I'm inviting you up to my apartment and you're turning me down?" She smirked. "Who are you?"

I chuckled as I turned off the engine and followed her up to her apartment.

Chapter Twenty-One

Kinsley

As soon as we stepped inside my apartment, I pulled out one of the kitchen chairs and told him to sit down while I went to the freezer and filled two small Ziploc bags with ice.

"This might hurt a little." I smiled as I put the bag of ice over his eye.

"Ouch." He flinched.

"Hold that while I tend to your hand."

I placed the second bag of ice over his swollen knuckles and held it there.

"What's your dad going to say when he sees you?" I asked.

"The same thing he always does. 'Get your shit together, son. You're thirty years old. You're disgracing the Calloway name.'"

I brought a chair up in front of him and sat down while I kept the ice bag on his hand. Our eyes met, and a feeling washed over me.

"My dad died of a heroin overdose when I was six and my mother is an alcoholic."

"Kinsley, you don't have to—"

"I do. I had to grow up fast. Faster than any child should ever have to. I'd been taking care of her and myself since I was a kid. Not only was she an alcoholic, but she was a stripper, so she worked nights and slept all day. I got myself ready for school, made my own lunch, and got myself on the bus. When I'd come home, she'd already have a few drinks in her and would be passed out on the couch. I'd have to wake her up to get ready for work. We never had any money because once she paid the few bills she had, she'd blow the rest of it on alcohol."

"Kinsley, I had no idea. Was she ever violent?"

"No." I gave him a small smile. "She never cared enough to get violent. In fact, she never cared about me period. She forgot about my birthday on several occasions because she was either too drunk or passed out. And when she did remember, she'd throw ten dollars at me and tell me to go buy myself something nice. She even missed my high school graduation because she was too hungover and couldn't get out of bed. Even though she promised me she'd be there."

Chase took the bag of ice off his eye and set it on the table.

"Why did you wait so long to leave?"

"It took me years of working to save up enough money. I started working at the antique shop when I was sixteen and I saved every dime I could. After a month of walking to work because I didn't have any other way of getting there, Mrs. Buckley gave me her husband's car because she said she it was time to give it away and I could use it."

"Mrs. Buckley sounds like a very sweet woman."

Chase Calloway

"She was." I smiled. "She was very generous and the kindest person I'd ever met. She wished she could pay me more, but the truth was, the antique shop wasn't doing that good and she was in a lot of debt. After she passed away, I found I had enough money saved to at least get me here and get a place, and I'd figure out the rest when I got here. But then I met Henry and I had this vision of the two of us living this happy perfect life in California. I wanted him to come with me, but he and his dad owned a roofing company and he couldn't leave. So, like an idiot, I stayed and ended up working as a waitress in a greasy diner."

"Of course you stayed. You loved him."

"I thought I did, but looking back on it, I fell in love with the idea that someone could actually love me." I looked down. "Before I left, I tried waking up my mom, who was passed out on the couch. She stirred and mumbled, 'Not now, Kinsley.' So I'm sorry if you think that I'm a coward for leaving a note."

He placed his finger under my chin and slowly lifted it until our eyes met.

"Don't apologize. You're not a coward. I had no idea your life was like that. And don't you ever doubt that someone could love you. You fought your way through life because you knew you deserved better. And now look." A smile graced his face. "You're here in California, living in this nice apartment, and you've made great friends. This is your life now, Kinsley, and you made it. You! Nobody else, and you should be so proud of yourself."

"Thanks, Chase."

He brought his hand up to my face and lightly stroked my cheek as he stared into my eyes. He slowly leaned forward until his lips were pressed against mine. I closed my eyes and let the sensation of the warmth run through me. He slightly pulled back and cupped my face with both his hands and I smiled, letting him know I didn't want him to stop.

"You're so beautiful," he whispered as his lips met mine once again.

Our tender and unsure kiss turned passionate as our lips moved in sync with each other's and his tongue met mine. A rush of excitement jolted me down below, and even though this was the last thing I wanted, I didn't care. We both stood up from our chairs, our lips never leaving one another's as he swept me up in his strong arms and carried me to the bedroom. He laid me down on the bed as his mouth devoured my neck while he fumbled with the buttons on my shirt until he unbuttoned the last one. A soft moan escaped me as his tongue slid over my lips, down to my collarbone and in between my breasts. He wasted no time, as my hands tangled in his hair, making his way down to the waistband of my pants, unbuttoning them and sliding them off me, exposing my black lace panties.

A growl erupted inside his chest as he stood up and stripped out of his clothes, revealing his perfect God-given package that made me swallow hard. He took a condom from his wallet, tore the corner of the package with his teeth, and slid it over his hard cock. The corners of my mouth curved upwards as he leaned over me and kissed my lips. Placing his hand underneath my back, he unhooked my bra, sat me up, and removed it along with my shirt. He stared at my breasts for a moment before laying me back down and taking each one in his mouth as I softly moaned in pleasure. Making his way down to my panties, he gripped the sides of them with his fingers and seductively pulled them off as his tongue explored my most sensitive area.

I arched my back in ecstasy at the skill this man possessed. With one finger dipped inside me and his tongue exploring my clit, he brought his other hand up to my breast, gently squeezing it and taking my hardened nipple between his fingers. Several moans escaped me as I was on the brink of an amazing orgasm.

"Come for me, darling," he spoke in a low tone.

The sensation was incredible. Something I'd never felt before with Henry. I was lost in a world of euphoria as my body trembled and a warmth rushed through me.

"God, that's beautiful," Chase whispered.

My heart was rapidly beating as he crawled up me until his lips reached mine. The feel of his muscular body against mine was overwhelming as was the feel of his hard cock at my opening. In one soft movement, he was inside, and my body willingly opened itself up to him, welcoming him in every way possible. A moan escaped his lips as he pushed deeper until he was buried inside me. He slowly moved in and out, preserving our moment and giving me the greatest pleasure of my life. As I wrapped my legs tightly around his waist, his thrusts became faster and harder, satisfying both of us with each stroke. Our lips danced together until I threw my head back and vocally let him know that he once again pleasured me in a way no other man had done before.

"Yes. Fuck yes!" he shouted as he slowed down and brought his mouth to mine while he came.

We both lay there, me underneath him while he collapsed, and the warmth of his breath shot against my neck. Once we both regained our breath, he pulled out of me with a horrified look on his face.

"What's wrong?" I asked.

"The fucking condom broke. Look. Please tell me you're on birth control."

"Shit. No. I'm not. I took the last of my pills a few weeks ago and I haven't seen a doctor here yet. But don't worry, I'll go first thing tomorrow and get the morning after pill. I have up to seventy-two hours to take it."

"So you've taken it before?" he asked.

"Once, and trust me, it works."

He climbed off the bed and went into the bathroom. I slipped into my robe and headed to the kitchen for a glass of wine. God knew I desperately needed it after that. And I wasn't talking about the condom breaking.

"I should get going," Chase spoke as he walked into the kitchen, buttoning up his shirt.

"Yeah. I think you should."

I set down my glass of wine and walked over to him, lightly running my finger across his bruised eye.

"Does it hurt?" I asked.

"A little bit, but I'll be fine." He smiled. "I'll pick you up around seven forty-five tomorrow since we need to stop at the drug store. Is that okay?"

"That's fine." I lightly smiled.

He leaned over and kissed my forehead.

"I hope this doesn't make things awkward between us," he

spoke.

"Nah. It was just sex. No big deal. Look at it this way," I spoke to lighten the mood. "When I want it, I know who to call."

"You can give me a booty call anytime." He winked. "I'll see you in the morning. Sleep well."

"You too."

Chapter Twenty-Two

Chase

Having sex was the best part of my life and it always put me in a fantastic mood. So why wasn't I? I drove home asking myself that very question over and over again. Sex with Kinsley was amazing. So amazing that the condom broke. In all my years of having sex, I'd never had that happen.

As soon as I got home, I pulled the condom box from my nightstand and examined it. Shit. The condoms expired three months ago. What the fuck! This was a brand new box I'd just picked up last night. I threw it onto my nightstand, changed into a pair of black pajama bottoms, and poured myself a scotch. I took it out to the patio and stared at the water as the moonlight glistened down on it. What the hell was my problem? Why did I feel like I was in a god damn funk? I'd finally had sex with Kinsley. It was my dream since the day my eyes laid sight on her. I'd won. Then why was it that I felt like such a loser?

The next morning, I arrived at Kinsley's house promptly at seven forty-five. Just as I was about to get out of the car, she came walking out of her apartment.

"Good morning," I spoke.

"Good morning," she replied as she climbed in my car. "What's in the bag?"

"A box of condoms."

"Oh, so now you're carrying the whole box with you? Don't want to run the risk of running out too soon?" She smirked.

"No." I smiled as I glanced at her. "I'm taking it back to the drugstore. They're expired. That's probably why it broke."

"Oh. You didn't notice the date before you bought them?"

"I never look at the date. I just assume they're fresh. God knows they probably restock every other day. Did you sleep well?"

"I did. How about you?"

"Yeah. I did," I lied.

"Let me see your eye," she spoke.

As soon as we were at a stoplight, I removed my sunglasses.

"Ouch." She brought her hand up to my face. "Your dad is going to be asking questions."

"I know. I'll come up with something on the spot. I always do." I smirked as I put my sunglasses back on and took off from the light.

We reached the drugstore, and while Kinsley went to go get the morning after pill, I returned the box of condoms.

"Can I help you?" the saleswoman asked.

"I need to return this box of expired condoms."

"Do you have a receipt?"

"No. I don't usually keep the receipts for condom

purchases."

"Then how do I know you didn't buy these before the expiration date, used a couple, and now are exchanging them for non-expired ones?"

I couldn't help but let out a laugh.

"Sweetheart, it's obvious you don't know who I am. I don't use just a couple. I use the whole damn box and rather quickly. I just bought these a couple days ago."

Kinsley walked up to the counter and stood next to me.

"You don't have proof you bought them a couple of days ago, and without a receipt, I can't take them back."

"Listen, darling. This woman and I had sex last night and the damn condom broke because it was expired. Do you understand the danger of selling expired condoms? Because it broke, she had to get the morning after pill."

"Two forms of protection is the way to go, sir. Personally, I wouldn't have had sex with her if she wasn't on birth control."

I stood there and took in a deep breath, for I could feel the heat rising in my body.

"I didn't know she wasn't on birth control," I spoke softly through gritted teeth.

"Then you shouldn't be having sex with her if you don't know her that well."

"Again, it's obvious you don't know who I am."

"Oh for fuck sakes." Kinsley grabbed the expired box of condoms, walked over to the trash can, and tossed them in.

"Ring up the new box, please. This is absolutely ridiculous." She reached in her purse and threw some cash on the counter. "Have a good day." She grabbed the new box of condoms and threw them at me. "Let's go. We're going to be late and I don't want to have tell your father that you were in a heated discussion with the salesgirl at the drugstore over a damn box of expired condoms."

"Someone's grumpy this morning. Did you take your pill?" I asked.

She held it up to me, popped it in her mouth, and chased it down with the bottle of water she'd bought. I pulled into the parking garage of Calloway Tech and we both took the elevator up.

"Have a good day, Miss Davis."

"You too, Mr. Calloway. I can't wait to hear what Daddy has to say about that nasty bruise." She smirked as she continued down the hallway.

"Looks like someone is in a good mood despite that nasty-ass bruise on that beautiful face," Lexi spoke as she followed me into my office.

"Good morning, darling."

"So what happened last night after you took Kinsley home?"

"Nothing. She put some ice on my hand and eye," I spoke as I wouldn't look at her.

"Oh my God, you slept with her!" she voiced loudly.

"Who did he sleep with?" Steven asked as he walked into my office.

"Kinsley!" Lexi answered.

"Bro, good job." Steven smiled as he walked over and tried to fist bump me.

"Will the two of you knock it off. I don't want to talk about it."

"Oh, Chase. What happened?" Lexi asked with a disapproving tone.

"As much as I want to stay and hear the juicy details, I just came to drop this file off and now I have a meeting to get to before your dad has my head. Fill me in later." He walked out of my office and shut the door.

"Spill it, Calloway. There's something you're not telling me," Lexi spoke as she took a seat across from my desk and folded her arms.

"I don't know. It was just weird."

"Sex with Kinsley was weird?" She arched her brow.

"No. Sex with her was amazing. It was after."

"I don't follow you."

"I left her place, went home, and found myself in a funk. I can't explain it, Lexi." I got up from my seat and paced around the room. "I'm always in a fantastic mood after sex, but last night, I wasn't. I was in a not-so-good mood."

"Wow, Chase. I think you've had feelings for her all along and last night sealed the deal."

"Don't be ridiculous. I don't have feelings for women and you know it. Not even for Kinsley."

"So how did you leave things? You have to see her every day. If you hurt her, Chase, I swear to God…"

"I didn't hurt her." I scowled. "We both agreed that we wouldn't let things be awkward between us."

"So she doesn't want anything more now that she's had the Chase Calloway sizzle stick."

"Jesus, Lexi. And no, she didn't lead me to believe she did. But, if she does, I'll have to set her straight. In fact, take her to lunch today and get some information from her about last night. I'll expect a report when you get back."

"She's my friend. I'm not doing that."

"And I'm your best friend in the world and your boss and I just gave you an assignment. If she wants more, then I'll have to make a plan on how to let her down gently."

"Well, if that's the case, then you better wait and do it when she leaves here, or else Daddy Calloway is going to be pissed as hell."

"I can handle my father. Just do it."

"Can't wait to hear what he says about that bruise." She smiled as she strolled out of my office.

Chapter Twenty-Three

Chase

As I was sitting at my desk, I couldn't stop thinking about the way Kinsley grew up. Her mother was a horrible and piss poor excuse for a woman and a parent. Not too far off from my own mother. I owed Kinsley the money for the box of condoms, and to be honest, I wanted to see her. So I walked down to my father's office, knowing damn well I was about to receive his wrath.

"Hello, beautiful." I smiled as I pulled some cash from my wallet.

"Hello." She batted her beautiful blue beauties at me.

"Here's the money for the box of condoms."

"Thank you." She took it from me with a smile.

Suddenly, my father's door opened.

"Chase. Please step your bruised face into my office."

Rolling my eyes, I walked in and took a seat.

"Care to explain what happened?"

"Some idiot punched me, so I punched him back."

"What did you do? Have sex with his girl?"

"No." My brows furrowed. "It was just a misunderstanding. He was a total douche."

"Was Kinsley involved?" he asked.

"No. Why would you ask me that?" My brows furrowed.

He turned his laptop around, which displayed a video of the events of last night.

"See, there's my temp standing next to you at a club. Now I'm going to ask you one last time, what happened?"

"I didn't know Kinsley was at the club. I was there with Alex and Steven for a guys' night out and she was there with Lexi. I saw her dancing on the dance floor with some douchebag and he had his hands all over her ass. It was totally inappropriate, so I intervened and pulled her aside. I explained to her that he could be a rapist, murderer, or kidnapper, and that if anything happened to her, you'd blame me because I was there. Then the douche walked over to us and I politely told him to go away and that's when he punched me, as you can see in the video."

"Okay then. That's good enough for me. I believe you did the right thing by getting her away from that guy."

"Seriously, Dad? You're not mad?" I asked in shock.

"No. You possibly saved her from making a mistake and I probably would have done the same thing. I'm actually surprised you cared enough since the two of you don't seem to get along."

"Well, she works for the company and I suppose she's not that bad."

"I swear to God, Chase, if you slept with her…" He pointed at me.

"I didn't." I put my hands up. "I drove her home and that's it," I lied. "Are we finished here? I have work to do."

"Yes. We're finished. Stay out of trouble, and I mean it." He scowled.

I walked out of his office and stopped at Kinsley's desk.

"I didn't hear any yelling." She smirked.

"That's because he was cool with my saving you from the douche-looking guy."

She rolled her eyes. "You don't know that he was a douchebag."

"He had his hands all over your ass when you were dancing. That makes him a douchebag. And another thing, I can't believe you let him do that." I cocked my head.

"Like you said, I was letting my party girl out." Her brow raised. "You act like you're jealous. Are you jealous, Mr. Calloway?"

"Fuck no. Why would I be jealous?"

"Because some stranger had his hands all over my ass and I wouldn't let you."

"For the record, darling, my hands were all over your ass and other delicious parts of your body. Have you forgotten already? And you better be very careful with your answer."

"I haven't forgotten, but that was after the fact." She smirked.

"You can rest assure that I was in no way jealous. I'm not the jealous type."

The phone rang and she placed her hand on the receiver.

"I'll talk to you later," she spoke.

As I walked to my office, I gave serious thought about her jealousy accusation. Fine, I'd admit that I was a little jealous when I saw the douche-looking guy all over her. But it was only because I hadn't had her first. That was what I chose to believe, even though another part of me was disagreeing.

****

Kinsley

Things were a little slow at the office. Mr. Calloway left for the afternoon, and I was all caught up on my work.

"It's lunch time!" Lexi smiled as she approached my desk. "How about some Thai food?"

"Sounds good." I grinned.

I grabbed my purse and the two of us headed to the Thai place around the corner.

"Thanks for helping Chase out last night with the ice. I asked him if he put ice on it as soon as he got home and he said you made him when he drove you home."

"No problem. To be honest, I didn't trust him to do it himself. You know how stubborn guys are."

"For sure." She smiled. "How are the two of you getting along?"

"We're getting along. Has he told you anything?"

"About what?" Lexi narrowed her eye.

"About last night."

"All he said was that you helped him with the ice. Why? Did something else happen between the two of you?"

I sat there, biting down on my bottom lip, debating whether or not to tell her.

"Did you sleep with him?"

"Yes." I sighed. "It just happened. It was in the heat of the moment."

"Okay. That's understandable, but you told me you'd never sleep with him."

"I know." I rolled my eyes.

"So how are you feeling about it or him now?" she asked.

"I don't know. I saw a different side of him last night, and I'll admit it was nice, but I can't let myself feel anything, and I won't. I just got out of a yearlong relationship and I don't trust men, especially Chase. Plus, I came here to find and reinvent myself and the last thing I need is to get wrapped up in some guy. I was never known as Kinsley Davis. People always referred to me as that poor girl whose mother was an alcoholic. Or that poor girl whose father overdosed on drugs. Or Henry's girlfriend. That's how I grew up, as 'that poor girl.' I want people to see me for who I really am and that's Kinsley Davis. I can't be me until I find me and detach from the 'that poor girl' label."

"I'm so sorry, Kinsley." She reached over and placed her hand on mine. "And I totally agree with you. You need to find and love yourself first." A small smile crossed her lips.

Just as we finished lunch and headed back to the office, my phone rang.

"Hello," I answered.

"Kinsley, it's Carl. Your car is ready. You can pick it up anytime."

"Thanks, Carl. I appreciate it. I'll be by after work to get it."

"Great. See you then."

I walked Lexi to her desk and popped my head into Chase's office to see if he was in there.

"Hey." I smiled as I saw him sitting at his desk.

"Hello, beautiful. What brings you by?" He grinned.

"My car is ready. Do you think you can drop me off after work so I can pick it up?"

"Sure. Just swing by here before you leave."

"Thanks, Chase."

"No problem. I'll see you later."

Chapter Twenty-Four

Chase

"Lexi," I yelled from my office. "Can I see you for a moment?"

She walked into my office and shut the door.

"I know what you're going to ask, so I'll just tell you. She doesn't have feelings for you."

"She said that?" I asked as I narrowed my eye.

"Yes."

"Impossible. Women always have feelings for me."

"In case you haven't noticed, Kinsley isn't like other women."

"Maybe not, but she's still a woman, and after sex with me, their feelings intensify."

"Not with Kinsley. And why the hell do you seem disappointed? Isn't this what you wanted? Now you don't have to worry about it."

"I'm not disappointed. I'm relieved. Thank you."

"You're welcome. Can I get back to work now?"

"You mean shopping online for new clothes?" I arched my brow and pursed my lips.

"And?" She smiled as she walked out of my office.

It was five o'clock when Kinsley stepped into my office looking as beautiful as ever.

"You ready?" I asked as I got up from my seat.

"Yes. I can't wait to get my car back."

As we were driving to get her car, she glanced over at me.

"What are you doing tonight?" she asked.

"I haven't decided yet. Why are you asking?"

"I don't know. I just thought maybe you'd want to come over and put those new condoms to use." She smirked.

"Kinsley Davis." I looked over at her with a wide grin on my face. "Are you letting your party girl out again?"

"Yes, Mr. Calloway. I am. Is that a problem?"

"No. No problem at all. What time should I be over?"

"Eight o'clock. And bring a pizza." She smiled.

Shit. My cock was already getting hard. I pulled into the parking lot of the auto repair center and Kinsley got out of the car.

"See you later." She winked with a smile.

I shook my head in disbelief. What happened to her? Then it hit me, and I slowly nodded my head with a smile on my face as I headed home. I had hooked her. She was becoming addicted just like I knew she would. As long as it was only sex she wanted, I was willing to give her as much of it as she needed.

****

Kinsley

I was a little shocked myself that I invited Chase over for sex. This wasn't me. Or was it? California was bringing out a side in me that I never knew existed. Why not? It was only sex and I had needs. After last night's performance, and not being able to get it out of my head, I wanted round two. I could do this sex-only thing. I was strong enough. Plus, all I had to do was keep thinking about what Henry did to me and it would be easy peasy.

Eight o'clock rolled around and there was a knock at the door. When I opened it, Chase was standing there holding a pizza box.

"Dinner is served." He grinned as he stepped inside.

"Thanks. I'm starving."

"You look sexy," he spoke as his eyes stared at me from head to toe in my satin robe.

"Thank you." The corners of my mouth curved upwards.

He went into the kitchen and set the pizza down on the table. As I was reaching up to pull some wine glasses from the cupboard, I felt two hands grab my hips from behind and a warm sensation against my neck.

"You look more delicious than the pizza does." His lips pressed against my bare flesh.

A light moan escaped my lips as his hands reached inside my robe and kneaded my breasts. I slowly turned around and our mouths met, our lips tangling with each other as I gripped the bottom of his shirt and pulled it over his head. The fire below was roaring at full force and I couldn't wait for him to put it out. His hands untied my robe and he slipped it off my shoulders, exposing my naked body underneath.

"Fuck, I'm so hard," he moaned as his tongue trailed along my neck.

I fumbled with the button on his pants and successfully pulled them off his hips as he dipped a finger inside me and I gasped.

"First I'm going to make you orgasm this way. Then you'll have another one with my mouth, and then a third one with my cock buried deep inside that beautiful pussy," he softly spoke.

"What makes you so sure I will?" I smirked as I bit his bottom lip.

"Oh fuck, Kinsley. Trust me, you will."

He worked my insides like nobody ever had before. The buildup was coming as I moaned in pleasure while my hand stroked his cock.

"Now you'll come," he moaned as he placed his thumb on my swollen clit and worked his magic. The incredible feeling took over me as my nails dug into his flesh and a rush of warmth poured out of me.

He didn't let me come down from orgasm number one before he got on his knees and his mouth was pressed against me. My hands tangled through his hair as his tongue explored every inch of my most sensitive area.

"Oh my God!" I shouted and threw my head back as another orgasm raced through me.

He stood up and I handed him the condom wrapper as he opened it and I helped him roll it over his hard cock.

"Fuck," he moaned before his mouth smashed into mine.

He lifted me on the counter and my legs wrapped tightly around him. In one hard thrust, he was inside me, and like last night, I took every inch of him in. After a few thrusts, he lifted me from the counter and carried me to the couch, where he took me from behind. Our moans grew louder as each thrust became faster and harder. My fingers gripped the back of the couch as my body fell into its third satisfying orgasm.

"You feel so good, baby," he moaned as he continued moving in and out of me.

Suddenly, he halted, and a satisfying moan erupted inside him as he came. He placed his hands over mine and softly kissed my back as we both slowly regained our breath.

"I've worked up quite an appetite," he spoke as he pulled out of me and disposed of the condom in the bathroom.

"It didn't break, did it?" I asked as I went into the kitchen and slipped my robe on.

"No." He laughed. "Everything was intact."

After he slipped his pants back on, and I poured the wine, we took a seat at the table and began eating our pizza.

"Lexi told me you've never been in a relationship," I spoke.

"Nope. Never." He took a bite of his pizza.

"Why? If you don't mind me asking."

"I have my reasons."

"And you're not going to share those reasons, are you?" I asked.

"No. I'm not. I'm a firm believer that you don't need to be in a relationship to be happy."

"Your dad and Penelope seem happy," I spoke.

"He's unhappy more than he is happy. I don't think one single person can make another happy long term. Life is about adventure and the thrill of spending time with people on a short-term basis. For example, with me, sex comes easy, but loyalty doesn't. Sure, I'm loyal to my circle of friends, but I couldn't guarantee I'd be with just one person. You of all people should understand that after what Henry did to you. He couldn't stay loyal. It's not who we are anymore. We're a generation of hook-ups instead of relationships. You don't have to love someone to feel good. You can get instant gratification with sex."

Wow. Did he really just say that to me? He was more fucked up than I thought he was.

"I'm sure you're not raring to get into a relationship with someone. He broke your heart and I'm sure you don't want to feel that again."

"You're right, I don't, but there are people out there who won't do that to the person they love," I spoke.

"Perhaps, but it's rare," he spoke.

"What was it like growing up for you?" I asked.

"Why?" He narrowed his eye at me.

"I told you my story, so now I want to hear yours."

"I don't talk about my childhood with anyone."

"Not even me?" I smiled.

"Not even you, sweetheart."

Chapter Twenty-Five

Chase

I wasn't ready to tell her anything about my childhood. The fact that she asked made me think she was trying to get closer to me and I couldn't have that.

"Okay then. Thank you for the sex and the pizza." She grinned as she took her plate and mine to the sink.

"What do you mean? Are you kicking me out?" I asked with irritation.

"I am. I got what I needed and now you're free to go."

"You're serious, aren't you?" I got up from my chair.

"I'm very serious, Chase. We hooked up, had dinner, and now I'm going to take a bath. I'll see you tomorrow at the office."

"Yeah. I'll see you tomorrow." I furrowed my brows.

What the fuck just happened? I thought to myself as I climbed in my car and drove off. She seriously couldn't be mad at me because I wouldn't tell her about my childhood. I honestly didn't think she was that type of person. She didn't seem mad, but her abruptly kicking me out told me otherwise.

"Hello," Lexi answered.

"Are you home?"

"Yes. Why?"

"I'm on my way over. I need to talk to you."

"It sounds serious."

"It is. I'll see you in about twenty minutes."

"The door's unlocked. Just walk in," she spoke.

I pulled into her driveway, threw the car in park, stepped inside the house, and headed straight to the bar she and Ben had in their living room.

"What's going on?" Lexi asked as I poured myself a glass of scotch.

"I'll tell you what's going on. I had sex with Kinsley and she kicked me out."

"What?" She laughed.

"It isn't funny, Lexi."

"Calm down, Chase, and tell me exactly what happened."

"She asked me to come over for sex and she told me to bring a pizza, so I did. We had amazing sex first and then while we were eating, she asked me about my childhood. I told her I don't talk about it with anyone, including her, and she said okay and told me to leave. She said she got what she wanted and I was free to go. Do you believe that?"

"Isn't that what *you* do?" Lexi cocked her head.

"Exactly!" I pointed at her. "It's what *I* do. I think she was pissed because I wouldn't tell her about my childhood."

"Maybe a little. But I think you're reading too much into it. Did she seem upset?"

"No! She was smiling the whole time. She said she was going to take a bath."

Lexi snorted, and I gave her a stern look.

"Listen, Chase." She walked over to me and put her arm around me. "She obviously wants to get to know you. It doesn't mean she wants a relationship. But friends know things about each other. She told you about her childhood, so she expected you to do the same."

"I don't talk about it and I don't talk about her." I threw back my drink.

"I know you don't, but maybe it wouldn't hurt to tell Kinsley. Just because you tell her doesn't make her your girlfriend. It doesn't put the two of you in a relationship."

"It's none of her concern, Lexi. The only thing between us is sex."

"Then if that's the case, why are you so pissed off she asked you leave?"

"Because it was childish of her, and to be honest, I'm disappointed in her. I didn't take her for that type of woman."

Laughter escaped Lexi's lips.

"That wasn't childish behavior, Chase. That was her telling you if you didn't want to talk about your childhood, then she was going to make better use of her time instead of wasting it on someone who won't open up. Especially right after sex."

"And taking a bath is making better use of her time?" I arched my brow.

"Apparently to her it is." She laughed.

"I'm glad you find all this amusing."

"Karma's a bitch. Isn't it? Finally." She raised her hands in the air. "A woman who stands up for herself where you're concerned. I never thought I'd see the day."

I rolled my eyes as I threw back the last of my second drink and set the glass down on the bar.

"I need to go home. I'll see you tomorrow morning." I kissed her cheek.

****

Kinsley

Sex with Chase was unlike anything I'd ever experienced in my life, and my body craved more of him. But I couldn't let it happen again. I thought maybe, just maybe, he'd open up a piece of himself to me, that maybe I was special. Stupid girl, right? I was no different from all the other women he slept with, and in the back of my mind, I knew it. Even though I wasn't looking for a relationship or to get attached to someone, I thought he trusted me enough to tell me something about himself.

I lay in the tub, the hot water soothing my soul. Tears started to fill my eyes and I hadn't a clue why. Maybe I did, but I couldn't admit it. I did the right thing by kicking him out. He wasn't going to know everything about me and I nothing about him. Maybe the other women he slept with didn't care, but I did. If I'm going to have sex with someone, I want to at least know about them. I shouldn't have invited him over, but I wouldn't give back those three mind-blowing orgasms he gave me for anything.

The next morning, I walked to my desk, set down my purse, and grabbed Mr. Calloway his coffee.

"Good morning, Mr. Calloway." I smiled as I set the cup on his desk.

"Good morning, Kinsley. Before I forget, Penelope and I are having a barbeque at the house tomorrow and we'd love for you to come."

"I'd love to."

"Excellent. It starts at four o'clock. I'll text you the address."

"Thank you, Mr. Calloway." I smiled.

I walked back to my desk and began doing my work for the day.

"Kinsley, I forgot to give you these when you were in my office. Can you take them over to Chase?"

"Sure." I swallowed hard.

I nervously walked down to this office, gripping the files tightly in my hands. When I approached Lexi's desk, she wasn't there, but Chase's door was open.

"She's running an errand for me," he shouted from behind his desk.

Slowly turning around, I swallowed hard and stepped into his office.

"Your father wanted me to give these to you." I handed him the files.

"Thanks. How was your bath last night?" he asked as his brow raised.

"Fine."

"Just fine? It should have been spectacular since you kicked me out to take one. Had you asked, I would've joined you." He grinned.

"I'm sure you would have, but you served your purpose to me and I was done. There was no need for you to stay any longer than necessary." The words flew out of my mouth.

"Served my purpose?" His eye narrowed.

Okay, maybe that wasn't the best choice of words, but they just came out faster than I could think.

"You know what I mean. I asked you over for sex and pizza. We had both, you didn't want to talk, and I wanted to take a relaxing bath."

"Aha!" He pointed at me. "So you did kick me out because I wouldn't tell you about my childhood! I knew you were pissed."

"I wasn't pissed, Chase. You have every right not to tell me if you don't want to. There was nothing else to talk about, so why stay?"

"Chase, bro. Oh, hello, Kinsley." Steven smiled. "I can come back." He pointed to the door.

"No need. I was just dropping off some files," I spoke before walking out of his office.

I could tell it bothered the hell out him that I kicked him out last night. Good.

Chapter Twenty-Six

Chase

I grabbed my surfboard and headed down to the water, dying to catch some waves and not think about how I had to attend my father's barbeque. I didn't invite him to my party, so I didn't understand why he felt the need to invite me to his. I sat on my surfboard, waiting for the next wave to hit, and thought about Kinsley, wondering what she did last night. Why the fuck did I even care? I was still pissed off at her for telling me that I served my purpose. Who the hell did she think she was?

After showering and running some errands, I drove to my father's house in the Hollywood Hills. As I walked through the door, I saw Penelope walking up the stairs.

"Nice of you to make it, Chase." She smiled. "Your father will be pleased."

"Thanks, Penelope. I wouldn't have missed it for the world," I spoke in a sarcastic tone.

I headed towards the patio, pushing my way through the crowd of people who were gathered in the living area. As I stepped onto the patio, I looked around to see if Steven and Lexi were here yet. Just as I pulled out my phone to text them, my eyes diverted over to the bar area, where I saw Kinsley talking and laughing with Adam Bancroft, a total douchebag whom I'd known for years. *What the hell is she doing here and why is she talking to him?* I thought to myself.

"Well, well, look who's here." I smiled as I walked over to the bar.

"Hi, Chase." Kinsley smiled.

"Chase, my man." Adam grinned as he patted me on the shoulder. "Long time no see. How have you been?"

"Hello, Adam. I've been great. Thank you. How's Mary doing?"

"We aren't seeing each other anymore."

"Sorry to hear. She was such a lovely girl. I didn't know my father invited you," I spoke to Kinsley. "I'm surprised you didn't mention it."

"He invited me yesterday and we didn't really talk."

"No. I suppose we didn't," I spoke. "Well, it looks like the two of you are having a fun conversation judging by all the laughter I saw, so I'll let you get back to it." I walked away with an attitude.

I grabbed two glasses of champagne from the tray one of the waiters was carrying around, downed one, and started on the other as I turned and watched Kinsley and Adam chatting it up again. I didn't like her body language. She was flirting.

"Jealous?" Lexi spoke as she walked up and stood next to me.

"Of course not. Why the hell would I be jealous?"

"Then why are you standing here staring at them like you're

ready to kill someone?"

"Don't be ridiculous." I finished off my second glass of champagne. "I was actually looking for my dad. Have you seen him?"

"Last time I saw him, he was talking to Mr. Baine."

"Sydney is here?" I cocked my head.

"Yeah. Why?"

"I thought the two of them had a falling out."

"I don't know. They were looking pretty chummy to me," she spoke.

"Why the hell is Kinsley talking to him?" I asked as I narrowed my eye. "Can't she tell what a douchebag he is?"

"You're a douchebag and she talks to you." Lexi smirked. "I always thought Adam was hot. They kind of look cute together."

"What the hell is the matter with you? You're her friend. Go talk some sense into her. And no, they don't look cute together. She can do better."

"You mean like you?" Lexi's brow arched.

"Of course, but only if I'm looking for a relationship. Which you know damn well I'm not and never will."

"If you say so." She sighed and walked away.

"Chase, there you are," my father spoke as he walked over to me.

"Hello, Dad. Why is Kinsley here?" I asked, still staring at her and Adam engaged in a conversation.

"She's my secretary. Why wouldn't I invite her?"

"She's your temp and you've never invited the temps to one of your barbeques."

"She's with us for at least two months. Do you have a problem with her being here? I thought the two of you were getting along now."

"We are. I just wondered, that's all."

"Why are you staring at her and Adam?" he asked.

"I'm not staring." I glanced over at him.

He narrowed his eye at me and was about to say something when Penelope shouted his name from a few feet away.

"We'll talk later. Go enjoy yourself. There are plenty of beautiful women here." He winked.

Indeed, there were. Everywhere I looked, I saw beautiful women, dressed in tight short dresses and bikinis that barely covered their assets.

****

Kinsley

After having a long but great conversation with Adam, I mixed and mingled with some of the guests from the office that were at the party. To me, this was amazing. I never thought in a million years that I'd be invited to parties like this. I glanced over at the beautiful infinity pool and saw Chase with two women, one on each side of him. He was in the pool, leaning up against the edge with his arms extended around them. A feeling erupted in the pit of my stomach. A feeling I didn't like. I took in a deep breath and walked over to them.

"What's going on over here?" I smiled.

"Hello, Kinsley." Chase grinned. "I'd like you to meet Karina and Renee."

I gave them each a small smile.

"Where's Adam? The two of you seemed to be attached at the hip." He smirked.

"He had to make a phone call," I spoke.

"Would you like to join us? I'm afraid, though, I only have two arms."

"Umm. No. That's okay. I wouldn't want to intrude on your little *ménage a trois*."

"Darling, the more the merrier." He grinned. "Right, ladies?" He glanced at each of them.

"Yeah. The more the merrier." Karina smiled.

I wanted to vomit as I rolled my eyes and walked away. And to think I slept with him. Jesus, what was I thinking? That he was a hot and gorgeous man? That he had the body of Adonis? That I knew he would be incredible between the sheets? Yeah. That was exactly what I was thinking. I sighed as I walked over to where Lexi was talking to one of our co-workers, Dana.

"Hey, you." Lexi smiled. "I saw you talking to Adam. What's going on?" She grinned.

"Nothing." I grinned back. "Actually, we're going on a date tomorrow night."

"Good for you!" Lexi high-fived me. "He's a nice guy and he's hot."

"He is. We seem to have a lot in common, but I did tell him I wasn't looking for any type of relationship and he said he wasn't either. He just got out of a three-year relationship."

"Well, I'm glad you're meeting new people." She smiled as she hooked her arm around me.

"Hello, ladies." Ben smiled as he hooked his arm around both me and his fiancée. "How about we get some food?"

After getting our food, we took a seat at an empty table where Adam joined us. While we were talking, Chase walked over and sat in the empty seat next to me.

"May I join you?" He smiled as he sat down.

"What happened to your little *ménage a trois*?" I raised my brow.

"I got bored." He grinned.

"Still nobody special in your life, Chase?" Adam asked.

"And lose the title of Los Angeles' sexiest and most eligible bachelor?" He smirked.

"I guess you're right." Adam chuckled.

"So, what happened between you and Mary? I thought the two of you were getting married?"

"We decided to call it quits," he replied.

I sat between them feeling very uncomfortable and in disbelief that Chase would even ask him about his prior relationship.

"Who cheated?" Chase asked.

"Nobody cheated."

"So that girl I saw you with in Vegas who wasn't Mary was just a friend?"

The look on Adam's face turned serious as he glared at Chase.

"Yeah. She was just a friend."

"Of course. What happens in Vegas stays in Vegas." He winked.

"I know you're the expert on that," Adam spoke.

"Not really. What or who I do never stays in Vegas." Chase grinned. "I have nothing to hide. I'm an open book."

"You are not." I laughed.

"Is there something going on between the two of you?" Adam asked as his eye slightly narrowed at us.

"Other than the fact that we've had sex, no, nothing," Chase spoke and I wanted to fucking throat punch him.

"And when was this?" Adam asked.

"A few days ago." Chase smiled.

I sat there with a lump in my throat and a sick feeling in my stomach. The anger that resided in me was ready to unleash.

"Okay then. Listen, Kinsley, I better get going. I have somewhere else I have to be in a while. It was nice meeting you and I'll be in touch. See ya around, Chase."

"Of course. Let's do dinner one night and catch up," he shouted as Adam walked away.

I turned to him and began hitting his arm several times. He backed away as he grabbed hold of my hand.

"What the hell are you doing?" he asked in a calm tone.

"Why did you tell him we had sex?!" I angrily spoke through gritted teeth.

"He asked."

"No, he didn't! He asked if anything was going on between us, and all you had to do was say no!"

"I did say no, besides us having sex. What's the big deal?"

"We were supposed to go out on a date tomorrow and now you ruined it!"

"Oh. Well, if he's that insecure, then that's his problem. Besides, you don't want to go out with him anyway. He's a cheater. I saw him in Vegas with a woman, and trust me, they were not just friends. Need I remind you that he had a fiancée at the time? And considering what you went through with Henry, I just saved you some heartache. So, you're welcome." He smiled.

I stared at him while taking in three deep breaths to try and control myself from killing him.

"Stop telling people we had sex or I'm going to tell your dad!"

"You're going to tell my dad what?" He chuckled.

"That we had sex! Twice!" I got in his face.

"Now, Kinsley. Don't do anything rash." He put his hands up.

Chapter Twenty-Seven

Chase

Kinsley got up from the table and walked away. I found out she and Adam were going on a date because Lexi slipped and told me. I couldn't let that happen. I didn't want her to get hurt. I knew Adam, and he would ultimately hurt her.

"What did you do to Kinsley?" Lexi spoke as she sat down next to me and shot me an evil look.

"I did nothing to her."

"Then why did I just see her stomp away all pissed off?"

"I may have told Adam we slept together."

"What the fuck, Chase! Why would you do that?"

"Because he's a cheater. She doesn't need to be going out with him."

"That's not for you to decide." She cocked her head with a narrowed eye. "Wait a minute. You couldn't stand the thought of her going out with him."

"You're right. I know him and he's a douchebag," I spoke.

"No. No. No." She shook her head. "You can't stand the thought of her going out with anyone besides you. You're jealous."

I sighed. "I am not jealous, Lexi. I don't do jealousy. How many times do I have to tell you that?"

"I don't care what you say, Calloway. If you didn't care or weren't jealous, you wouldn't have made it known the two of you slept together. You knew it would bother Adam."

"So what?" I shrugged.

"You can't control other people's lives. Shit. Either you step up to the plate and tell her that you like her or leave her the hell alone!"

Lexi stood up and walked away. I sat there with my drink in my hand, giving my actions some serious thought. Fine, maybe I shouldn't have told Adam that Kinsley and I had sex. Maybe I needed to apologize. I got up from my seat and went to look for her.

"Hey, Chase." Alexandria stopped me by placing her hand on my chest. "You up for a little fun?" She winked.

"I'll have to take a raincheck, sweetheart. I need to find someone and talk to them."

"Can't you find them after?" She smiled.

"No. I'm sorry." I removed her hand from my chest and walked away.

I searched the whole outside and couldn't find her.

"Hey, Steven." I placed my hand on his shoulder. "Have you seen Kinsley?"

"She left a while ago."

"She left? Did she say where she was going?"

"I'm assuming home. I don't know, bro. I didn't ask."

"Thanks." I sighed.

I left the party and drove to her apartment. I let out a sigh of relief when I saw her car in a parking spot. I knocked on the door and alerted her that it was me before she opened it.

"What are you doing here, Chase?" she spoke with an irritated tone.

"I need to talk to you."

"About what?" She cocked her head.

"Can I come in?"

"Fine." She sighed.

I stepped inside her apartment with my hands tucked into my shorts pockets and paced around the room.

"I wanted to apologize to you for earlier. I'm sorry I told Adam we slept together."

"Why, Chase? Why are you apologizing?" she asked.

"Because I saw it upset you and I wanted to say that I was sorry."

"What does it matter to you if it upset me?"

"You're my friend, Kinsley, and the bottom line is I shouldn't have said it."

"We're friends?" she asked as she took a seat on the couch.

"I thought we were."

"I was under the impression that I was just another notch in your bed post."

I walked over to where she was sitting and sat down next to her.

"I consider you my friend. We've had some pretty good times together." I smirked.

"You're referring to sex, aren't you?"

"Yes." I smiled.

"Then I am just another notch in your bed post."

I reached over and lightly grabbed her hand.

"No, Kinsley, you're not."

"Then why won't you tell me anything about you?"

"The only thing you don't know about me is my childhood and I'm not going there. I need you to respect that."

"You're wrong. I don't really know a thing about you except the fact that you're a sex addict and love beautiful women."

"First off, I'm not a sex addict. And yes, I do love beautiful women. Second of all, go ahead and ask away." I smiled. "I'll answer any questions you have except about my childhood."

"Did you always want to work for your dad's company?"

"My dad's company was nothing more than a computer sales company. It wasn't until I developed a program when I was ten that his company took off."

"Ten?" she asked in shock.

"Yes. Believe it or not, I'm actually tipping the scale between being highly intellectual and genius level. I graduated high school when I was sixteen, went straight to Stanford, where I met Alex and Steven, graduated before I was twenty-one, and then my father gave me an office and a high-ranking position at the company."

"So, Steven and Alex are older than you?"

"Just by two years. I'd actually been working for my father since I developed my first program. I coded, he paid me. I own half the company. That was the deal I made with him if he wanted me to continue developing systems and software for him. If it wasn't for me, he'd still be just selling computers."

"I guess you are very smart." She grinned.

"Career smart at least." I smirked. "He runs the company and my team and I develop the products."

"Why didn't you just work for him instead of going to college?" she asked.

"And miss out on the great college experience?" I smirked. "I wanted to continue to learn, especially with the way technology changed so much. Plus, I needed to learn about business. When my father retires, I'll be taking over the company."

"Did you play any sports?" she asked.

"Nah. Sports never interested me. The only thing I cared about was technology, until I moved to California and started surfing."

"So you were a geek and now you're a hot surfing geek?" She smiled.

"Yeah. I guess I am." I laughed.

I stared into her beautiful blue eyes, and in one uncontrollable movement, I found my hand stroking her cheek. She stared back, unsure if she was enjoying it or if she wanted me to stop.

"I'm sorry I ruined your date."

"It's okay. You did say he was a cheater."

I leaned forward and lightly brushed my lips against hers. I wanted her and I hoped she wouldn't say no. Her lips greeted mine and our kiss turned passionate. My cock was already hard and standing at full attention. If she didn't want to have sex, I needed to know now.

"Are you sure?" I asked as I broke our kiss.

"Yes. I'm sure." She smiled as she brought her hand up to my face.

Chapter Twenty-Eight

Kinsley

I lay in bed, three orgasms later, feeling elated. It was one a.m. and Chase went to get out of my bed when I grabbed his hand.

"Just stay. It's late," I spoke.

"Are you sure?"

"If I wasn't, I wouldn't have asked."

He gave me a small smile and climbed back in, wrapping his arm around me as I lay my head on his chest. Feelings. They were developing faster than the speed of light, and I was trying so hard to stop them.

"I have a question for you," he spoke.

"What is it?"

"How could you not think we were friends? After all, I did make sure you got home safely from my party, I stayed the night, and I made you coffee the next morning. I just don't do that for anybody."

"I don't know. I just thought you did those things because you were trying to get into my pants." I smirked as I lifted my head and smiled at him.

"True. I was." He smiled back.

I laid my head back down and listened to the beating of his heart.

"Kinsley, I just need to make it very clear that I don't want anything more. I mean, I like you and I love having sex with you, but that's all I can give. Nothing more. It's not who I am, and I think you know that by now."

"I do know that and I'm not looking for anything more either. I love being on my own, discovering who I am, and trying to find the best version of me."

"Well, if it makes you feel better, I like this version of you." He kissed the top of my head.

We both fell fast asleep, and when I woke up, I was lying on my side with Chase's arm wrapped tightly around me. I liked it, maybe a little too much. He was closed off. Sure, he opened up to me a little bit last night, but not about his mother or his childhood, and I believed that was where his relationship issues stemmed from. He was a playboy who flirted with anyone of the female gender. I could never trust him, even if we did get into a relationship. So, for now, I'd take what I could get from him until I was ready to be with someone.

****

One Month Later

The moment I climbed out of bed, I ran to the bathroom and threw up. I had hoped it was a one-time thing, probably from the Chinese food I ate last night. But it wasn't, and I had to call in sick to work. I felt bad because I only had two weeks left working for Mr. Calloway.

"It's okay, Kinsley. The most important thing is that you get better. Don't worry about it. I'll have Lexi fill in for you."

"Thank you, Mr. Calloway. I'll be there for sure tomorrow."

"Feel better soon."

I hung up the phone, lay on the couch, and turned on the TV. A few moments later, I received a text message from Chase.

"Dad said you called in sick. Are you okay?"

"I think that Chinese food we ate last night didn't agree with me."

"I'm fine."

"We didn't eat the same thing."

"Do you need anything?"

"No. I think I'm going back to sleep for a while."

"Okay. Text or call me if you need anything."

During the past month, Chase and I had been seeing each other a lot. We'd have dinner and then sex. The nights he wasn't with me, he'd go out to the clubs and party. I would go to my yoga class or hang out with Lexi and a few other friends I made. We'd go to the bars and I would get hit on by multiple guys, but no one I was interested in.

As the day went on, I felt better, so I took a shower and decided to clean my apartment. Six o'clock rolled around and there was a knock at the door.

"It's me, Kinsley," I heard Chase yell.

Opening the door, I saw him standing there holding up a brown bag.

"I've brought you some soup. How are you feeling?" he asked as he walked inside.

"Thank you. I'm actually feeling better."

"Good." He smiled as he took down a bowl from the cabinet and poured some soup in it. "I can't stay. I'm having dinner with my dad and bridezilla."

"Sounds like a fun time." I smirked. "Is there a special occasion?"

"It's Penelope's birthday this weekend, and since they're going on a trip and won't be here, dear old Dad thought tonight would be a good night to get together for dinner."

"Did you buy her a birthday gift?" I asked as he set the bowl of soup down in front of me.

"As much as it pains me to do it, I'm going to stop at the florist on the way and pick up some flowers."

"I like Penelope. She's really nice. I don't understand what you have against her," I spoke.

"I'm just not fond of her." He shrugged. "I better head out. I don't want to get yelled at for being late. You good?" He smiled.

"I'm good. Thanks again for the soup."

"No problem. I'm glad you're feeling better." He kissed the top of my head and then walked out the door.

I sighed. I promised myself I wouldn't fall for him, but I had.

I hated him going to the clubs and doing God knows what with other women. I hated myself for feeling like that, but I couldn't help it. I knew damn well he wasn't good for me. As a friend, yes. As a sex partner, yes. As a boyfriend/lover, no. I still needed to find out what his real issues were. I had asked Lexi about it, but she wouldn't say. She told me that when Chase was ready to tell me, he would.

The next morning, I woke up with the same feeling as yesterday. I cupped my hand over my mouth and ran into the bathroom. What the hell was going on? I was fine last night. I couldn't call in again and, with any luck, I'd feel better like I did yesterday, so I did my best to put on a smile and head to work.

"Good morning, Kinsley." Mr. Calloway smiled. "How are you feeling today?"

"I feel a lot better," I lied.

"You look a little pale."

"Still recovering, but I do feel better," I spoke.

"Glad to hear it. Would you mind stepping into my office for a minute? There's something I would like to discuss with you."

"Sure, Mr. Calloway."

I followed him into his office and took a seat while he shut the door. My sick stomach felt even sicker with worry that I did something wrong. Shit. What if he found out that Chase and I were sleeping together?

"As you know, Audrey is supposed to be back in a couple of weeks," he spoke.

"Yes. I know." I nodded.

"I spoke to her yesterday and it seems her fiancé got a once-in-a-lifetime job in New York, so they're moving there, and she will not be coming back to Calloway Tech."

"Oh." My brows furrowed. "I'm sorry to hear that."

"I would like to offer you the full-time position here at Calloway Tech as my personal secretary. You'd get a pay increase, full health benefits, a 401k plan, profit sharing, and a yearly bonus."

"Mr. Calloway, I don't know what to say," I spoke in utter shock.

"Say yes. I'd love to keep you, Kinsley. You're a bright woman and you do a very good job. Plus, you can handle my son and I wouldn't have to worry about his actions affecting you. You seem to be the only woman I've ever known who's immune to him." He smirked.

Shit. If he only knew.

"I would love to stay here at Calloway Tech." I smiled. "Thank you for this opportunity, Mr. Calloway."

"Excellent. I'll send your paperwork down to Human Resources and give the temp agency a call."

I thanked him again, and when I walked out of his office, Chase was walking down the hallway.

"I was looking for you. How are you feeling this morning?" he asked.

"Much better," I lied again. "Did your dad mention anything

to you at dinner last night about Audrey not coming back?"

"No. Why?"

"Apparently, her and her fiancé are moving to New York, so she's not coming back."

"Oh. Then I guess Daddy is going to have to find a new permanent secretary."

"He did already," I spoke.

"Wow. That was fast. Did he tell you who he hired?"

"Me." I smiled. "He just offered me the full-time position."

"I see. Congratulations."

"Thanks. I feel a lot better now, knowing I have a permanent full-time job."

Chapter Twenty-Nine

Chase

Fuck. I wasn't sure how I felt about my father making Kinsley a permanent fixture here. I did like seeing her every day, but when things between us start to go bad, it was going to be awkward. The feelings I'd developed for her over the past month were getting to me. I found myself always wanting to be with her. My mind wouldn't stop thinking about her, even when she was right down the hall. I was actually looking forward to her time here being up, because the less I saw of her, the sooner I could let us drift apart. I figured my father had forgotten what he told me a few weeks ago about creating a position at Calloway Tech for her. He never mentioned it after that day. Shit.

"Lexi, in my office, please," I spoke as I walked past her desk.

"What's wrong?" she asked.

"Have a seat. Kinsley just told me that my dad hired her permanently to be his secretary."

"What? What about Audrey?"

"Apparently, she's moving to New York with Dustin."

"Oh. Good for Kinsley." She smiled.

"It's not a good idea and now I don't know what to do."

Chase Calloway

"About what?" She cocked her head.

"About her."

"I'm lost here, Chase." She shook her head.

I let out a long sigh. "I was going to slowly let things fade between us when she left."

"Why?" Her eye narrowed at me.

"Because we've been sleeping together for too long now. We work together and see each other every day. It's kind of hard to forget about her when she's sitting right down the hall."

"So what you're saying is out of sight, out of mind?"

"Exactly!" I pointed at her. "How can I end things now that she's going to be working here full-time?"

"Why would you want to end things?" she asked.

"Because I feel like we're getting too close. I brought her chicken soup last night to her house. The other night when she stayed over, she left a few things in the bathroom. When I told her she left them, she said just to leave them there for when she stayed over again."

****

Kinsley

I walked over to Lexi's desk to tell her the great news, but she was in with Chase. I started to walk away until I heard my name. The door was slightly ajar, so I carefully listened. Tears started to fill my eyes when I heard the things Chase said. The sick feeling that was already in my belly intensified and my heart started racing. I couldn't listen anymore, so I went to my desk and composed myself the best I could. The feeling was too deep, and it sent me to the bathroom, where I vomited in the toilet a couple of times. When I returned to my desk, Lexi walked over.

"Hey." She smiled. "These are for Mr. Calloway to sign."

"Thanks. I'll give them to him." I gave her a small smile.

"Are you okay?" she asked with concern.

"Yeah. In fact, I'm great. I was going to walk over and see you. Audrey isn't coming back and Mr. Calloway offered me her job."

"Oh my God, Kinsley. I'm so happy!" She hugged me. "You accepted it, right?"

"Yeah. I did."

"Let's celebrate tonight. Dinner and drinks on me."

"Maybe another night. I'm still not feeling well."

"Oh. Okay. Another night it is, then."

The work day was finally over, and I couldn't wait to get home. The words Chase spoke went round and round in my mind like a carousel. All I wanted to do was take a relaxing hot bath, get in my pajamas, curl up on the couch, and binge watch something.

I got home after being stuck in traffic due to an accident for over an hour, threw my keys down on the table, and started the bath water. I stepped into the bubbly tub and sank down until the water reached my neck. Closing my eyes, I started to relax, until Chase crept into my head. Tears started to stream down my face as I recalled the conversation I heard earlier. The way he was slowly going to let things fade once I left Calloway Tech, how we were getting too close, and the big deal he made about me leaving a few things at his house. Once again, my heart broke in two. I hated myself for getting involved with him. I knew better. I told myself that he would hurt me at some point, but I would be able to handle it. Was this handling it? Sitting in a bathtub crying my eyes out?

Once I started to turn into a prune, I got out of the tub, dried off, and slipped into my pajamas. Walking into the kitchen, I grabbed a gallon of chocolate ice cream from the freezer, a spoon from the drawer, and took it over to the couch, where I started binge watching *Sex and The City*, Season One. I'd seen it a million times, but it was always my go-to when I had a heartache series.

As I made my way to the halfway point in the carton of ice cream, my phone dinged with a text message from Chase.

"Hey, I was thinking I could come over tonight. What do you say?"

"No."

"Why not?"

"I'm not feeling well."

"Oh. I'm sorry to hear that. Do you need anything? I can bring you over something."

"No. I have everything I need."

"Okay. Get some rest and I'll see you tomorrow."

I didn't reply back, and he was never coming over again. I

was putting an end to our whatever the fuck you wanted to call it, letting it fade, just like he wanted it to.

The next morning, I woke up sick again. I was attributing it to the gallon of ice cream I ate before bed. Like the past two mornings, I vomited, got dressed, tried not to think about how crappy I felt, and headed to work.

"Good morning, beautiful." Chase smiled as he stopped by my desk. "How are you feeling?"

"Like crap. Thanks for asking," I spoke with a hint of attitude in my tone.

"Still? Maybe you should go see a doctor."

"So he can tell me I have a virus and to let it run its course? No thanks."

"Somebody is moody today," he spoke.

"Is there something you needed, Chase? I have a lot of work to do."

"No. I just stopped by to see how you were."

"You could have just texted me," I spoke.

"Perhaps I should have." He shot me a look. "Have a good day, Miss Davis."

"You too, Mr. Calloway."

****

Chase

What the hell was her problem? I went into my office and

threw my phone across my desk.

"Good morning, boss." Lexi smiled as she walked into my office and set my coffee on the desk.

"What's so good about it?" I growled.

"Whoa. What's your problem this morning?"

"Why don't you ask, Kinsley, what her problem is?"

"I'm sensing the two of you had a fight," she spoke.

"I texted her last night and told her I was thinking about coming over. She said no and that she wasn't feeling well. I just stopped by her desk to see how she was feeling and she had an attitude. She told me I could have just texted her instead of walking over."

Lexi snickered.

"Really?" I cocked my head.

"Sorry. She hasn't been feeling good. Cut her some slack."

"Then she needs to go to the doctor," I spoke.

"That's not for you to decide. It's her decision."

"She doesn't have to take it out on me because she doesn't feel good."

"Just let her be, Chase."

"Trust me, I am." I picked up my coffee cup and took a sip.

Kinsley had had an attitude with me before, but this time, it was different.

Chapter Thirty

Kinsley

I escaped the rest of the day without seeing Chase. I was sure he was pissed off about my attitude towards him this morning, but I didn't care. Let the fading begin. I went home and fell asleep on the couch, waking up at ten thirty in disbelief I'd slept that long. This wasn't normal for me, and if I wasn't feeling well again tomorrow, I'd have to go see a doctor. Something wasn't right.

The next morning as I sat at my desk, I googled medical centers near me, found one, and called the office to see if I could get in the same day. Fortunately, there was an available appointment at four o'clock, so I took it.

"Excuse me, Mr. Calloway." I peeked my head inside his office.

"Come on in, Kinsley. What can I do for you?"

"Is it okay if I leave early today? I have a doctor's appointment at four o'clock."

"Still not feeling well?" he asked.

"No. I thought I was getting better, but I guess not."

"That's fine."

"I can come back to the office after if you want."

"That's okay, sweetheart. Go get yourself checked out and then go home and rest." He smiled.

"Thank you."

I walked out of his office and shut the door, only to find Chase standing by my desk.

"There you are. How about dinner tonight at my place?" he asked.

"Sorry, I can't."

"You have other plans?"

"Yes. Actually, I do."

"I see."

"How about tomorrow night, then?" he asked.

"I have yoga tomorrow night."

"After?" his eye narrowed at me.

"I'll be too sweaty and tired," I replied.

"Okay." He sighed.

"You have all of L.A. to entertain you, Chase."

"You're right. I do, Kinsley. I'll talk to you later." He walked away with an attitude.

When it was time for me to leave for my appointment, I grabbed my purse, said goodbye to Mr. Calloway, and headed to the medical center.

"Hello, Kinsley, I'm Dr. Harrison. It's nice to meet you."

"Nice to meet you as well." I smiled.

"So, tell me what's been going on with you."

"I've been sick to my stomach the past few days and I've been exhausted."

"How many times are you vomiting in a day?" he asked.

"Two to three times. Usually in the mornings. When I get home from work, I'm so exhausted that I feel like I need to take a nap. Yesterday, I slept for four and a half hours, got up, changed into my pajamas, and went to bed for the night."

"Are you sexually active?" he asked.

"Yes." I bit down on my bottom lip in embarrassment.

"Is there a chance you could be pregnant?"

I swallowed hard as a sickness fell into the pit of my stomach.

"No. We've been using protection. There was this one time over a month ago where the condom broke, but I went the next morning and took the morning after pill. So no, I can't be pregnant. I was on the pill three months ago, but since I moved here, I hadn't gotten them refilled because I needed to see a doctor first."

"Okay. We'll draw some blood first and then I'll examine you," he spoke before calling his nurse into the room.

I sat there on the table while my blood was being drawn, scared to death at the possibility that I could be pregnant. But the morning after pill is so effective, so there was no way I could be. After Dr. Harrison checked my throat, ears, and glands, he left the room and said he'd be back as soon as my test results were ready. I pulled my phone from my purse as I waited and noticed a text message from Chase.

"I was just in a meeting with my dad and he told me you had to leave for a doctor's appointment. How did it go? What did the doctor say?"

I didn't reply to his text message because I had nothing to tell him. Besides, what business was it of his? He felt we were getting too close, so why did he even bother to pretend he cared?

The door opened and Dr. Harrison walked in.

"I got your test results back, Kinsley." He stared at me.

"And?"

"You're pregnant."

"I'm sorry, Dr. Harrison, but I can't be. I took the morning after pill. That's what it's for, to prevent pregnancy."

"Only if you haven't already ovulated. It takes a while for your body to get back on track after stopping the pill."

"Great." Tears started to fill my eyes.

"You have options," he spoke.

"I know I do, but an abortion isn't an option for me."

"I'm happy to hear that. I'm going to give you the name and number of an obstetrician. She's very good and used to be a colleague of mine. Her office is up on the third floor. Give her a call in the morning and set up an appointment. You'll need to start your prenatal care as soon as possible."

"Thanks, Dr. Harrison."

Before leaving the building, I had to stop into the bathroom and throw up. This wasn't morning sickness, it was straight nerves. What the fuck was I going to do now? I was pregnant, and Chase Calloway was the father. Shit. The timing and the father couldn't be worse.

When I got home, I crawled up on the couch like a child. My head was spinning with all sorts of thoughts. How was I going to tell him? How would he react? I already knew how he'd react and it wasn't going to be pretty. He couldn't even commit to a relationship, let alone a child. Maybe I shouldn't tell him that the baby was his. I could lie and say I had a one-night stand with someone. He wouldn't believe me. Oh my God, what about Mr. Calloway? How the hell was I going to tell him. He just hired me for the full-time position. Now I was pregnant and going to have to go on maternity leave. My life was falling apart in front of my very eyes and I didn't know what to do.

I heard my phone ding, so I got up from the couch and pulled it out of my purse.

"I asked you a question and I don't appreciate being ignored," Chase wrote.

"Sorry. I just got home. I have a virus, just like I thought I did."

"At least you found out what's wrong. If you need anything, text me."

"Thanks."

I couldn't tell him I was pregnant, especially over text. Face to face was going to be hard as it was, and I needed to prepare myself to be as strong as I could be. I placed my hands on my belly and looked down. I needed to accept the fact that I was going to have a baby and that I'd be raising him or her alone.

Chapter Thirty-One

One Week Later

Chase

Kinsley had been in a mood all week and I was sick of it. Besides her damn attitude towards me, we hadn't had sex. Every time I suggested it, she turned me down. What the hell was going on with her?

"Lexi, in my office," I shouted from behind my desk.

"You don't have to shout."

"Shut the door and have a seat."

She stood there with her hands on her hips and her head cocked.

"Please," I spoke. "Do you know what the hell is going on with Kinsley?"

"What do you mean?"

"She hasn't had sex with me in over a week. She's been telling me no and her attitude sucks."

"Maybe she doesn't want to have sex with you anymore," she spoke.

Chase Calloway

"Impossible." I threw my pen across the desk. "Is she seeing someone and you're not telling me?" I narrowed my eye at her.

"Not that I know of. If she was, I'm pretty sure she'd tell me. We went to yoga class last night and she was fine."

"None of this makes sense. I didn't do anything."

"Maybe she's letting your relationship of convenience fade." She arched her brow. "And why is this bothering you? You were going to do the same damn thing to her. So you should be happy she's behaving like this. It lets you off the douchebag hook. Why don't you just ask her?"

"I guess I'll have to, and she will tell me the truth."

"Be careful, Chase. You might not want to hear the truth."

I finished the program I was working on and didn't leave the office until eight p.m. I hadn't spoken to Kinsley because I didn't want to deal with her attitude at the office. But now I was ready, so I showed up at her apartment unannounced.

"What are you doing here, Chase?" she asked as she opened the door.

"We need to talk and you're going to tell me what the hell your problem is," I spoke in a stern voice as I stepped inside her apartment.

****

Kinsley

I spent the last week trying to figure out how to tell him about the baby, but I couldn't. A part of me was scared, but I knew he had the right to know. I did a lot of soul searching during the last few days and accepted the fact that this was real and I was going to be a mom. Strength had to become my best friend for I would not be the kind of mother mine was to me.

"What are you talking about?" I sighed.

"You have been unbearable. You don't want to see me, you won't have sex with me, and whenever I try to talk to you, you act like you hate me. What the fuck did I do to you? Because if I did something, I sure as hell have no clue what it was."

"I just think it's best that we don't see each other anymore outside of work."

"And why not?"

"Because."

"Damn it, Kinsley. 'Because' isn't an answer!" he shouted so loud that I flinched and lost control.

"Isn't this exactly what you wanted?" I shouted back.

"What the hell are you talking about?"

"I overheard your conversation with Lexi in your office. The one about us getting too close and how you were going to let things fade between us."

"You heard that?"

"Yes, I did."

"You knew I couldn't be anything more than just a sexual partner with you. I told you that from the start!" He pointed at me. "And you agreed. You said you weren't looking for anything else."

"Oh no." I shook my finger at him. "You aren't putting the blame on me. I never once hinted to you that I wanted anything more."

"I'm not going to stand here and argue about this with you," he sternly spoke.

"Of course you're not, because you're the one with the issues. So anti-relationship. Scared to death to get involved with someone for one reason or another. Have to sleep with every woman you lay eyes on and don't give a damn how bad you hurt them. You walk around L.A. like you're God's greatest gift to the world, but in reality, you're just a scared little boy trapped inside a man's body hiding behind all your mommy issues!" I shouted.

He stood there and stared at me as anger overtook him.

"You don't know a damn thing about my mother, and how dare you say that to me. I'm done with you!" he yelled as he pointed his finger at me. "Done!" He headed towards the door and placed his hand on the doorknob.

"I'm pregnant," I spoke in a calm manner.

He froze and slightly turned his head.

"What did you just say?"

"I'm pregnant."

"Is it mine?" he asked, refusing to look at me.

"Of course it's yours. You're the only man I slept with."

He turned around and faced me. My heart was rapidly beating, and I felt sick to my stomach. So sick that I felt like I was going to pass out, so I sat down on the couch.

"When did you find out?" he asked in an authoritative tone.

"Last week when I went to the doctor."

"You told me he said it was a virus."

"I was in shock and I was trying to figure out a way to tell you."

"Are you keeping it?"

"Yes. I'm keeping it."

"I don't want to be a father, Kinsley. Not now, not ever. Fuck! How did this happen? You took the morning after pill."

"Apparently, I had already ovulated."

"I can't believe this is happening." He placed his hands on his head.

"Me either. But it is. I've thought a lot the past week and nobody will ever know you're the father. So, you don't have to worry about your precious reputation. I'm going to raise this baby alone and I'll have papers drawn up relinquishing you of your parental rights."

"You'd do that?" he calmly asked.

"Yes."

"And what are you going to tell people when they ask who the father is?"

"I'll tell them I had a one-night stand with someone."

"I can give you a lump sum of money. You won't have to

worry about not being able to support it."

"I don't want anything from you, Chase, and I certainly don't want your money. I'm going to raise this baby by myself and I'll make it work like I've done my whole life."

"Are you sure this is what you want?" he asked.

"Yes. This baby didn't ask to be created and I sure as hell am not turning my back on him or her."

"I hope you understand that I can't be a part of this."

"I do understand, and I don't want you to be a part of this."

"Okay. As long as we're in agreement. I have to go." He walked out the door.

Chapter Thirty-Two

Chase

I shut the door to her apartment and inhaled a deep breath, taking in the fresh night air. This was too much to handle and I didn't know what to do. I couldn't call my friends because they were never to know that I was the father of Kinsley's baby, and I certainly couldn't tell my dad. I was on my own with this one. As long as Kinsley stood by her word, my life wouldn't change and no one would ever know. She was strong, a lot stronger than me, and she could do it.

I drove home and went down to the beach, staring at the dark ocean water with a bottle of scotch in one hand and the other tucked into my pants pocket. Bringing the bottle up to my lips, I took a large drink, trying to calm the nervousness that resided inside me. I sat down in the sand and wished that Kinsley would have lied to me and told me someone else was the father.

"Why? Why are you doing this to me?" I spoke as I looked up at the starry sky. "You know how I am. You know I run and you know I never let myself get involved. I forgave you years ago after she left me. I thought that was my ultimate punishment. But now this? Why would you do that?" I took another drink. "The kid didn't ask for this and he or she certainly didn't ask for me to be its father. Is this another punishment for the way I live my life? Because if it is, you've really outdone yourself on this one." Once again, I brought the bottle up to my lips and finished off the scotch that was inside it.

Falling back into the soft sand, I thought about Kinsley, and the reasons I was so upset she rejected me. The reasons why I kept sleeping with her. The reasons why I cared when she was sick, and the reasons why I didn't want her seeing anyone else but me. I closed my eyes to stop the tears from stinging and before I knew it, the sun had risen.

****

One week later

The past week had been total hell. Kinsley and I didn't utter a word to one another. In fact, I barely saw her the whole week. I purposely stayed away from my father's office, which wasn't hard since he was gone on a business trip. I was sitting at my desk, when there was a knock at the door.

"What is it, Lexi?"

"It's not Lexi," Kinsley spoke as she opened the door. "She's at lunch."

"What can I do for you?"

"I have the papers for you to sign."

"Papers?" I asked in confusion.

"The ones relinquishing your parental rights." She handed me the envelope. "I hired an attorney and explained to him the situation. He said the courts could deny it, so he made sure everything was properly indicated."

"As in?"

"You're giving up rights to the child voluntarily, I agree, and that I want no money for support. There's a few other things listed. You'll see them when you read over the documents. You should have your attorney look at it as well."

"I will. Thanks, Kinsley. How are you feeling?"

"Tired, but fine. I just wanted to drop those off. I need to grab something to eat before my lunch hour is over."

"Yeah. Sure. Enjoy your lunch."

She walked out of my office as I held the large envelope in my hands. I didn't have time to look over the documents, so I put the envelope in my briefcase for later.

****

Kinsley

This was for the best and I knew it. He didn't want to be a father and I wasn't going to force him to be. I wasn't going to let my child grow up like I did. I was an accident and my father didn't want me, but my mother forced him to be a small part of my life, and to be honest, I think I would have been better off if I never knew him.

Shortly after I got home from work, there was a knock at my door.

"Delilah." I smiled.

"Hello, dear. I brought over dinner. I hope you don't have plans."

"Actually, I don't have any plans. Come in."

Chase Calloway

She stepped into my apartment with her large red casserole dish and brown-handled paper bag and went into the kitchen.

"I made a chicken dumpling casserole and a fresh homemade loaf of bread."

"Sounds delicious. That was so sweet of you to do that."

I reached up and pulled down two plates from the cabinet.

"We haven't had much of a chance to talk lately," she spoke. "Plus, I wanted to check up on you and see if you were all right."

"I'm fine." I smiled as we sat down at the table.

"One night last week, I was going for a walk and I heard a lot of shouting coming from the apartment. Then, when I was on my way back, I saw Chase leaving and he didn't look happy. I haven't seen him back here since."

"Chase and I aren't seeing each other anymore."

"I'm sorry to hear that. You two made such a cute couple."

"We weren't a couple, Delilah. We were more—"

"Friends with benefits?" She smiled.

I couldn't help but laugh. "You know what that means?"

"Honey, I may be old, but I'm up to date on what you young people do nowadays."

"Yes. We were friends with benefits."

I loved Delilah. She was so easy to talk to and was so wise. I could tell her anything and I knew she'd take it to her grave.

"I'm pregnant, Delilah."

Her face lit up with excitement as she grabbed hold of my hand.

"Kinsley, that's wonderful news. Congratulations. I take it Chase is the father?"

"It's complicated. He is, but nobody can ever know."

"Why?" She cocked her head in confusion.

"He doesn't want the baby and he doesn't want to be a father. So I had papers drawn up relinquishing him of all his parental rights. I won't force him to be something he doesn't want to be, because in the long run, it'll hurt the child."

"That's true. I take it you know this from personal experience?"

"Yes." I looked down as I played with my food.

"You're a brave and fearless woman, Kinsley Davis. You don't have to worry about me. I won't tell a soul and I'll be here to help you." She softly smiled.

"Thank you. I know I can trust you."

"He's frightened, that's all," she spoke. "Whatever happened in his past has a grip on him and it won't let go. I've seen the way he looks at you and I know he cares for you deeply, even if he doesn't admit it to himself."

"I don't think Chase Calloway is capable of caring for anyone but himself."

"He is, and I think he would make a good father. But, as long as he lets his past consume him, he will never truly live up to being the man he was meant to be."

"I know that. I just wished he did."

After we finished eating, Delilah helped me clean up and headed home.

"Thank you for dinner. It was delicious." I gave her a tight hug.

"You're welcome, dear. If you need anything at all, please call me."

"I will."

I shut the door and headed to the bathroom to take a bath. As I lay there, letting my mind wander, I thought about my mom. My pregnancy was something I should be sharing with her, but I didn't want to, and it saddened me. She wouldn't care anyway, and I could never trust her around my baby.

Chapter Thirty-Three

Kinsley

"Mr. Calloway, can I talk to you for a minute?" I asked as I stepped inside his office.

"Of course, Kinsley. What can I do for you?"

I took in a deep breath as I sat down in the chair across from his desk.

"I don't know how to say this," I softly spoke.

"You're not quitting, are you?" he asked.

"No. I'm pregnant."

He set down his pen and leaned back in his chair.

"Oh. I'm going to assume this wasn't planned."

"No, it wasn't."

"I didn't know you were seeing anyone."

"I'm not." I looked down in embarrassment.

"May I ask who the father is?" he spoke with the fear that I was going to name Chase.

"I had a one-night stand with a guy I met. I'm embarrassed

and ashamed."

"Please tell me that one-night stand wasn't my son."

"No. It wasn't Chase."

"Whew, you had me worried there for a minute. Well, thank you for telling me, and if there's anything you need, just ask me. I will support you in any way I can."

"Thank you, Mr. Calloway." I got up from my seat and headed towards the door.

"Kinsley?"

"Yes?" I turned around.

"Don't be ashamed. Accidents happen."

I gave him a small smile and walked out of his office. I could no longer hide the news from Lexi. She was my best friend and I felt like shit not telling her when I found out. But I couldn't. I wasn't ready for anyone to know.

It was lunch time, so I walked over to Lexi's desk.

"Are you ready?" I asked.

"Give me one second." She typed away at her computer.

"Kinsley." Chase nodded as he emerged from his office.

"Hi." I looked away as quickly as I could.

"Are the two of you going to lunch?" he asked.

"Yeah. We're heading over to the Chinese restaurant. Kinsley is craving their wonton soup." She smiled.

Chase glanced at me and a small smile crossed his lips.

"Hey, why don't you join us?" Lexi asked him.

Shit.

"Nah. It's okay. You two go and have girl talk."

"Kinsley doesn't mind. Do you, Kinsley?" she looked at me.

What the hell was I supposed to say? Yes, I do mind because I didn't want to be around him?

"No. Not at all," I lied.

"Are you sure?" he asked me.

"Why not? The more the merrier."

Little did he know that I was going to tell Lexi that I was pregnant. When we arrived at the restaurant, we were seated in a booth, which made it extremely awkward because I didn't know who Chase was going to sit next to. I tried to make it so I was the last one in the booth and I'd sit next to Lexi, but Chase had to go and be a gentleman and motioned for me to slide into the seat first before he sat down next to me. Shit. We placed our order, and as soon as our food was ready, I figured now was as good a time as any to tell Lexi.

"I'm pregnant," I blurted out as I picked up my spoon.

"What?!" Lexi exclaimed as she dropped her fork. She glanced at Chase and then back at me. "Is—"

"No." I shook my head.

"Did you know about this?" she asked Chase.

"No. I'm just as shocked as you are," he replied.

"Kinsley, who's the father?" Lexi asked.

"I had a one-night stand with some guy I met while running on the beach. We talked, went out for a couple of drinks, and it just happened."

"Why didn't you tell me about this guy?" she asked in disappointment.

"Because I was ashamed, and I didn't want you to think any less of me. It happened one time. He was from out of state. I didn't even get his last name."

God, I hated lying to her and it was killing me, but I had no choice.

"Did you know about this guy?" She cocked her head at Chase.

"No. Kinsley, I must say I'm a little shocked." Chase glanced over at me.

"What are you going to do?" Lexi asked.

"I'm having the baby and I'll raise him or her alone. I can do it." I smiled.

"Wow. I don't know what to say. Congratulations. You know I'll be here to help you every step of the way and I'm sure Chase will be too. Right, Chase?"

"Yeah. Sure," he spoke with a panicked voice. "Anything you need." He swallowed hard.

"Did you tell Mr. Calloway?" Lexi asked.

"I told him this morning."

"What did he say?" Chase asked.

"Not much. He told me if I needed anything to let him know."

****

Chase

"What happened between you and Kinsley?" Lexi asked as she followed me into my office when we returned from lunch.

"We aren't having sex anymore," I replied.

"Why?"

"She overheard us that day talking."

"Which day?"

"The one where I said we were getting too close and I was going to let things fade."

"Oh my God, why didn't you tell me?"

"I don't know." I shook my head. "I guess I didn't want to talk about it. She said some pretty nasty things to me."

"So that's why the two of you haven't really been talking here at the office. I knew something was going on. I got really scared there for a minute. I thought you were the father of her baby."

"Me? No way. No way in Hell."

"Yeah. That would be pretty bad if you were. I mean, you of all people shouldn't be a dad." She laughed.

"Excuse me?" I arched my brow. "Why not?"

"Because you're selfish and the only person you can love is yourself."

I narrowed my eye at her.

"What?" she asked. "Aren't you the one who goes around telling people that you're incapable of love?"

"Is the Edwards file ready yet?"

"Almost," she replied.

"Then get back to your desk and finish it!"

"Yes, sir. I'm not telling you anything you don't already know." She got up and walked out of my office.

After I left the office and drove home, I poured myself a drink, took the envelope with the papers in it, and sat out on the patio. I had just gotten them back from my attorney and he said everything looked good and I had nothing to worry about. As I pulled out the documents and read them over, my phone beeped with a text message from Kinsley.

"Hey, sorry to bother you, but I want to know if you signed the papers yet? I have to get them back to my attorney so we can finalize this."

"Not yet. I've been really busy with a new project. I'll sign them and give them back to you."

"Thanks."

"And for the record, you're not bothering me."

I set down my phone and placed my face in my hands. Kinsley was an incredible woman and I knew damn well what my feelings for her indicated. She was the first woman I'd ever met that somehow broke through the defensive wall I built around me and I didn't know how she did it. I picked up my phone and called a buddy of mine, Darius Cole.

"Darius, it's Chase Calloway."

"Chase, my man. How are you?"

"I'm good. Thanks. I need a favor from you, buddy."

"Of course. Anything."

"I need you to dig up some information on a woman named Kinsley Davis from Berkshire, Indiana. I need an address, friends, where she worked, etc."

"Sure. Let me see what I can find."

"Thanks," I spoke as I ended the call.

Chapter Thirty-Four

Kinsley

I pulled into the medical center parking lot and took the elevator up to the third floor. Upon entering suite 304, I signed in, filled out the new patient paperwork, and patiently waited for my name to be called. This was my first appointment with Dr. Nancy Morgan, the obstetrician Dr. Harrison recommended. This wasn't how I envisioned my first appointment. I had a vision that I'd be sitting here, hand in hand with my husband, just as excited as I was. I was a little nervous, but this was something I'd have to get used to, being alone on this journey. Lexi offered to come with me, but I knew she already had dinner plans with Ben and his family.

"Hi, Kinsley, I'm Doctor Morgan." She extended her hand with a smile.

"Hi, Doctor Morgan." I lightly shook her hand.

"I'm going to have you lie down and I want to do a quick ultrasound just to verify how many weeks you are."

I lay back as she pressed into my belly with the transducer and stared at the screen.

"I'm going to turn this up." She smiled. "See this?" She pointed to a small flashing dot on the screen. "This is your baby's heartbeat."

Tears started to fill my eyes as I stared at it.

"Wow," I spoke.

"You're about eight weeks pregnant." She cleaned the gel off my belly with a tissue and helped me up. "I'm going to start you on prenatal vitamins and you are to take one starting today. I see here you're single." She looked at my chart.

"Yes. I am."

"And the baby's father?" She glanced at me.

"He's not in the picture."

"That's okay." She smiled. "Try to live a stress-free life during this pregnancy. Of course, I don't have to tell you that stress isn't good for you or your baby. Are you active?"

"I run every morning at least three miles and I take yoga classes."

"Good. Keep it up. You want to keep your body as healthy as possible. Continue with the yoga as well. It will help keep your stress to a minimum and keep you centered." She smiled.

On my way home, I stopped at the grocery store to pick up a few things I needed. As I was in the produce section, picking out some apples, I looked up and saw Chase standing there.

"Hey." He lightly smiled.

"Hey." I continued placing the red apples in a bag.

"I see you're loading up on fruits and veggies," he spoke.

"Yep. I take it you're doing some shopping as well."

"Just picking up a few things. Steven is having a little get together. I went down to my dad's office and he said you left early for a doctor's appointment. Everything okay?"

Why the hell was he asking me? He didn't give a damn and this small talk was getting on my nerves.

"Yeah. Everything's fine," I spoke, deadpan.

"Good. I better get going. I'll see you tomorrow."

"Yeah. Have fun," I spoke.

Chase and I barely spoke anymore. When we did, it was strictly business at the office. He was a stressor in my life and the less I was around him, the better off I was. I had forgiven him for turning his back on me and his baby. I had no choice if I wanted any peace in my life. But just because I forgave him, didn't mean I had to be his friend. That was something we'd never be again.

****

Chase

Steven's get together was a bros' night at his place with me, him, and Alex. We played poker, kicked back some beers, ate snacks, and finished off a couple of large pizzas.

"Why didn't you tell me Kinsley was pregnant?" Alex asked.

"I don't know. I guess I didn't think about it." I shrugged.

"If you're not the father, who is?"

"Some guy she had a one-night stand with."

"Hell, had I known she was sleeping with someone other

than you, I would have fucked her myself." Steven grinned. "I would love to put my cock inside that beauty."

I swallowed hard as anger rose inside me and I tried to control myself.

"I bet that sexy mouth of hers could suck a dick like no other. You would know, Chase. Give us the details."

I got up, lunged across the table, and grabbed his shirt with both my hands.

"Don't you ever talk about her like that again," I growled. "If you weren't like a brother to me, I'd fucking flatten you right here."

"Chase, dude, calm down." Alex stood up and placed his hand on my arm.

I let go of Steven and walked away.

"What the fuck is your problem, bro?" Steven yelled. "We always talk about women like that."

"Not her!" I pointed at him in anger.

I walked out the patio door and headed down to the beach, taking a seat in the sand and listening to the roaring sounds of the waves.

"What's really going on, Chase?" Alex asked as he sat down next to me and handed me a bottle of beer.

Alex was always the reasonable one of the three of us and I knew I could trust him.

"I'm the baby's father."

"I somehow already knew that," he spoke.

"I told her that I didn't want to be a father and I couldn't, so she had papers drawn up for me to sign relinquishing my parental rights." I brought the bottle up to my lips.

"Did you sign them?" he asked.

"Not yet."

"Why not?"

"I don't know."

"I think you do know, but you're so scared that you can't admit it to yourself. I've known you a long time, Chase, and I've never seen you like you are when you're with Kinsley. Yeah, you were friends and fuck buddies, but I know it went beyond that. I think you need to talk to someone, like a therapist. There's nothing wrong with that. They'll be able to help you see things clearer."

"Maybe. Listen, please don't tell anyone what I told you. Kinsley and I had an agreement that no one would ever know I was the father."

"I won't." He hooked his arm around me. "But I will tell you something and I want you to listen to me very carefully. It doesn't matter how hard you are on the exterior, when you see your kid, you're going to feel something, whether you want to or not, and I'd hate to see you live a life of regret." He patted my shoulder and walked away.

I was up all night, tossing and turning. My life was perfect before Kinsley moved here and now it was nothing but a fuckery of a mess. The next morning, as I was sitting at my desk, my phone rang.

"Hey, Darius."

"Hey, Chase. I have that information for you. I'm sending it via email now."

"Thanks. I really appreciate it."

"No problem."

"By the way, this needs to stay between us."

"I figured that. No worries," he spoke.

I opened up my email and studied it. Picking up my phone, I booked a flight to Indiana.

"I'm heading out for the day, Lexi. Have a good weekend."

"You too, Chase."

Before I left the building, I walked down to Kinsley's desk.

"Hi. Is he in there?"

"No. He's been at a golf outing all day," she spoke.

"That's right. I forgot," I lied. "Well, have a good weekend."

"You too." She gave me an odd look.

I knew my father was out of the office, but I wanted to see her one last time before I left.

Chapter Thirty-Five

Chase

By the time I arrived in Indiana, it was late. I booked a room at the hotel airport, and come morning, I'd rent a car and drive to Berkshire, which was only about an hour and fifteen minutes away.

I was up early, rented a car, and headed out. While I was driving through the small town of Berkshire, I looked around at the dreaded scenery.

"Good God, now I know why she wanted to leave this place," I spoke to myself.

My first stop was at the greasy diner she worked at for breakfast. When I walked in, all eyes were on me. I stuck out like a sore thumb in this town.

"Hi," a young woman chomping on gum like an animal spoke. "Table for one?"

"Yes. Please."

She took me over to a booth by the window, and within a few moments, the waitress walked over.

"Hi, I'm Krista. Can I get you some coffee or juice?"

Ah, this must be her former best friend. I wasn't sure why her ex would want to sleep with that.

"Hello, sweetheart. "I smiled. "I'll have some coffee and an orange juice. Is it freshly squeezed?" I asked.

She laughed. "Umm, no. It's actually frozen."

"I see. Just coffee will be fine."

This place was a dump and I couldn't understand for the life of me why Kinsley would work here. She was right, it was a grease pit. I picked up the menu and cautiously looked it over. I was afraid to eat anything here.

"Here's your coffee." Krista smiled. "Are you ready to order?"

"Is your fruit plate fresh?" I asked.

"Judging by your looks, you're obviously not from around here."

"No, I'm not. I'm passing through."

She leaned in closer to me.

"I wouldn't touch the fruit plate if I was you." She winked.

"Okay, then. I'll have scrambled eggs and whole wheat toast, no butter."

"Good choice." She smiled.

"Do you have a second?" I asked her.

"For what?" She licked her lips.

"I'm looking for someone. Her name is Kinsley Davis."

"Kinsley? Why are you looking for her?" she asked in shock.

"We're acquaintances. I met her a while back and I wanted to say hi."

"Kinsley never told me she met anyone. Especially someone who looks like you. We used to be best friends, but she up and left town a few months ago. Nobody knows where she went off to."

"Krista!" the fat man in behind the counter yelled. "Quit the chit chat and get back to work."

"He was asking me about Kinsley."

"Kinsley? If you see her, tell her she's fired. That bitch was the only waitress I had scheduled and she never showed."

"Well, I can't say that I blame her."

"I'm sorry, but she's gone and I don't know where she is," Krista said.

"Thank you for your time," I spoke.

The diner wasn't crowded at all. In fact, there were only four people, including me, in the place. The door opened and a rugged-looking man who appeared to be in his mid to late twenties walked in.

"Hey, Henry." Krista smiled as she walked over and kissed him.

"Hey, baby."

He took a seat at the booth in front of me, sitting directly in my view. I studied him. He wasn't bad-looking, but nothing great either. Obviously, he and Krista were still getting it on.

Douchebag. Krista walked over to him, set down a cup of coffee, and then whispered in his ear. He looked up at me.

"Hey, Krista says you were asking about Kinsley."

"I was. Do you know her?"

"I sure do know her. How do you?" he asked with an attitude. "You're not from around here."

"No. I'm not, thank God, but I was looking for her to say hi."

"Like I asked, how do you know her?"

"I'm an acquaintance of hers. We met a while back. Actually, it was in this diner when I was passing through town. She was my waitress and I found her to be really nice. She told me to stop and say hi if I ever passed through here again."

"Well, she's not here. She left town," he spoke.

"That's what your girlfriend said. I guess I'll be on my way."

He glared at me as I threw some money down on the table. When I got up, I walked over to him, grabbed him by his shirt, and punched him in the face.

"That was for Kinsley, you douchebag," I spoke as I walked out, got in my car, and sped off.

I pulled into the driveway of the rundown house she called home. It was small and couldn't be any more than a thousand square feet. When I knocked on the door, an older woman answered it in a red silk robe with her hair up in a high ponytail, holding a drink in her hand.

"Hello, there. I'm looking for Kinsley."

"Well, hello there, handsome." She seductively smiled. "I'm afraid my daughter isn't here."

"Damn. I was really hoping to see her. May I come in and wait?"

"You can come in." She opened the door wider. "But you'll be waiting an awful long time. She left town a couple of months ago. I haven't heard from or seen her since."

I stepped inside the messy house and looked around.

"Can I offer you a drink?' she asked.

"Do you by any chance have scotch?" I arched my brow.

"Of course I do." She grinned as she went into the kitchen. "How do you know Kinsley?"

"We met one day when I was passing through town. I wanted to say hi and see how she was doing."

She poured some scotch in a red Solo cup and I was appalled.

"Sorry, all my glasses are dirty. But scotch is scotch, right?"

"Right." I hesitantly took the cup from her.

"Kinsley was the one who always kept the house clean. Since she left, I haven't been really keeping it up."

"I can see that. Where did she go?" I asked.

"I don't know. I woke up one day to a note saying that she couldn't stay here anymore and that she was leaving. I thought she meant she was going to live with her boyfriend Henry, but when I called him, he told me that they had a huge fight and he hadn't seen her since."

"Weren't you worried about her?"

"Nah. Kinsley is a smart girl. She can take care of herself. In fact, she was the one who always took care of me. Life was hard for us."

"I'm sure it was," I spoke as I once again looked around. "Is that normal for a child to take care of a parent? I could have sworn it was supposed to be the other way around."

"Excuse me?"

"Kinsley told me a little about you and your lifestyle. How you were always passed out drunk and never paid any attention to her."

"Like I said, life was hard for us. I may not have been the best mother, but I tried."

"And how exactly did you try? She had to get herself ready for school, make her own breakfast and lunch, come home to a mother passed out on the couch. For fuck sakes, you missed your own daughter's graduation. You made her feel like she didn't matter."

"It sounds to me like you and my daughter were more than just acquaintances. Who the fuck do you think you are coming into my home, dressed in your fancy expensive clothes, and talking to me like that?"

"I happen to care about your daughter. More than I can say for you."

"I love my daughter. I may not have always shown it, but I do. Kinsley is a strong girl and she got out of this dump. She left to make a life for herself instead of sticking around here ending up like me."

"Do you even miss her?" I glared at her.

"Of course I miss her. She's my little girl. But I can't begrudge her for wanting her own life. I get the feeling you know where she is."

"I do and I'm not going to tell you. Kinsley wants nothing to do with you. I had to come see all of this for myself."

"She doesn't know you're here, does she?"

"No. She doesn't."

"Is she okay?"

"She's fine and living the life she always wanted."

"Are you her boyfriend or something?"

"I'm a friend."

"Do me a favor. Tell her that I love her, I'm sorry for everything, and I miss her."

"You could have told her that yourself the day she left. She tried waking you, but you dismissed her, just like you've done her whole life."

"You need to leave now. You can see yourself out." She walked away with her drink in her hand and went into the bathroom, closing the door behind her.

Before I left, I wanted to see Kinsley's room. So, I walked down the hallway and looked into the first room on the left. That was when I saw Beatrice lying on her bed, the floppy-eared pink bunny Kinsley found in the street one day when she was eight years old. I remembered her telling me about it one night while we were lying in bed. She said that when she found her, she was covered in dirt and mud, so she brought her home, threw her in the washer, and when she pulled her out, she looked brand new. She told me that her biggest regret was forgetting to pack her when she left, so I grabbed her and left the house.

I was going to stay one more night, but I couldn't wait to get out of this town. Plus, there was no reason for me to stay here any longer, so I drove straight to the airport.

"Hi there, how can I help you?" the cute bubbly girl behind the counter asked.

"When is your next flight out to LAX?"

"Let me see." She smiled as she started typing away at her computer. "We have a flight that leaves in three hours. Would you like me to book you a seat?"

"Yes. First class, please."

"I'll need to see your driver's license, please."

I pulled my license out of my wallet and handed it to her. She took it from me, looked at it, and then up at me.

"Chase Calloway. Nice name," she flirted.

"Thank you."

"You're all set at Gate 22." She smiled as she handed me my ticket and my license back. "Have a safe flight, Mr. Calloway."

"Thanks. I intend to." I winked.

I was hungry, so I decided to sit down in a restaurant and grab something to eat since that breakfast I ate wasn't very appetizing. How could one fuck up scrambled eggs? I ended up at a place called The Brewhouse, which was right up my alley.

As I was sitting in the booth deciding what I was going to order, I noticed a man, woman, and their baby sitting at the table next to me. The child was crying, and the mother couldn't seem to quiet him down, so the father took him, and instantly, he stopped. I stared at them and watched how he handled his child. I could see the love pouring out of him as he made his child laugh.

Chapter Thirty-Six

Chase

Even though I got in late last night from the airport, I was up as the sun was rising and out on the water. I sat there, on my board, staring at the sunrise over the crystal blue ocean water. I needed to talk to Kinsley and I needed to do it today. It was time, and as scared as fuck as I was, I knew I had no choice. I waited until around one o'clock and then I headed over to her apartment. I grabbed the gift bag and the envelope containing the documents off the seat and walked up the stairs.

"Kinsley, it's me." I knocked on the door.

"Chase, what are you doing here?" she asked as she opened it.

"I need to talk to you. May I come in?"

"Yeah. I guess."

I set the bag down in the corner and handed her the envelope.

"I brought the papers back."

"Thanks." She took the envelope from me and took the documents out. "You didn't sign them?" She looked up at me.

"No. I didn't and I'm not going to."

"What?" she asked in confusion.

"Sit down, Kinsley. Please."

"Chase, what is going on?"

"I'll explain everything if you sit down."

I paced around the room for a moment, trying to work up the courage to talk to her about the things I never talked about. My heart was beating at a rapid pace and I was sweating profusely.

"Chase?"

I took in a long, deep breath.

"My mother and I were very close when I was a child. She was my world and I loved her so much. My dad was constantly working, and she was the one that was always there for me. We did everything together. She always put me first no matter what. Then one night, when she was on her way home from shopping with her friends, she was in a car accident and broke her back. I'd never seen her in so much pain and it frightened me. The recovery was long and hard for her, so the way she dealt with it was taking more pain medication than she should have. Once she was fully recovered, she continued taking pain pills, which led to other drugs; bad drugs. Right before my very eyes, she became a drug addict."

"How old were you?" Kinsley asked.

"I was eight years old at the time. My father put her in rehab for six months and we went and visited her once a week. She told me she was going to get better for me because she loved me so much and she hated me seeing her like that. She came home, and a couple of months later, she was back on drugs. At first, she hid it very well, but eventually, she spiraled downwards. She and my dad would argue every single day. Screaming and yelling at each other. I begged her to go back into rehab, and I asked her to do it for me because I loved her so much. I remember sitting on her bed one morning and her placing her hand on my face with tears in her eyes. She told me that she loved me so much and that she was checking herself back into rehab. She checked herself out after being there for a couple of weeks and I never saw her again. My father tried for a year to find her, gave up, and filed for divorce."

"Chase," she softly spoke. "I'm so sorry."

"I isolated myself and that was when I started coding and working on programs. It was a distraction from thinking about her. I was so angry that she would do that to me and I couldn't understand why. She said she loved me. You aren't supposed to do that to the people you love, especially your own child. My dad ended up marrying Greta, one of my stepmothers. She was kind and accepted me as her very own. She was my substitute mom and I loved her. A couple years after they were married, she was diagnosed with stage four uterine cancer, which quickly spread to other parts of her body, and she died within three months. My father couldn't stand to be alone, so he married three more times. Things never worked out and they would divorce. I would never get close to any of them, because if I did, I knew they'd leave."

I walked over to the couch and sat down next to her, placing my elbows on my knees.

"You were right about me being a scared little boy and hiding behind my mommy issues. It seemed like everyone I loved left, so I made a promise to myself never to get close to someone, out of fear they'd eventually leave. I couldn't take the heartbreak. That's why I live the way I do. It's easier for me that way."

She reached over and placed her hand on mine.

"I'm sorry you had to go through that."

"When you told me about the note you left your mom, it struck something inside me. That's why I said the things I did to you. And the reason I got so angry was because you're different from any other woman I've ever met. I can't explain it, Kinsley, but you've brought out feelings in me that I never wanted to have."

"Chase," she softly spoke.

"Let me finish. I really like you, Kinsley, and I have since the day I met you. Like I said, you're different from anyone I've ever met, and I want to be a part of your life and our baby's life. I'm not going to abandon either one of you." I lightly smiled.

"But what about your reputation? Your title of L.A.'s sexiest and most eligible bachelor?"

"That's all it is; a title. And now it can be changed to L.A.'s sexiest daddy." I grinned.

Kinsley let out the sweetest laugh.

"I wouldn't blame you if you hated me after the things I've said to you," I spoke.

"I don't hate you, Chase. I've liked you too since the first day I met you. It's just—"

"Kinsley, I know I have a lot to prove and I promise you that I will. I know you've been hurt by your mom, your dad, Henry, and Krista, but I can promise you that I'll never hurt you. I want to be with you and only you and I want to raise our baby together."

"Are you ready to be a father?" she asked.

"Are you really ready to be a mother?" I arched my brow.

"I don't know." She smiled.

"Exactly. I don't think anybody's ever really ready. I have something for you." I smiled as I got up from the couch and grabbed the gift bag.

"What's this?" She looked up at me as I handed it to her.

"Open it."

She removed the tissue paper from the bag and pulled out her bunny. Her jaw dropped as she stared at it and she looked at me with widened eyes.

"Beatrice. Chase, how—"

I knelt down in front of her.

"I paid a little visit to your hometown. Dreadful place."

"I told you it was. Why did you go there?"

"I wanted to see where you grew up."

"You went to my house?"

"I did, and I met your mother. She's—"

Kinsley put her hand up.

"You don't have to say it. I can't believe you went there. How is she? You didn't tell her where I was, did you?"

"No. I didn't tell her. I did tell her that you're living the life you always wanted. She wanted me to tell you that she loves you and she misses you."

Tears appeared in her eyes.

"She said you're a strong woman and she's happy you got out."

"Sounds like you had quite a talk."

I brought my finger up to her eyes and wiped away the tears that began to fall down her cheek.

"We had a brief chat and then she kicked me out."

"What?" She laughed.

"I tried to be nice, but she hurt you and that hurt me, so I let her know what a lousy mother she is. And I quote, 'Who the fuck do you think you are coming into my home, dressed in your fancy expensive clothes, and talking to me like that?'"

"Oh my God, Chase." She continued laughing.

"Can you believe she served me scotch in a red plastic cup?"

"I'm sure all three glasses in the house were dirty," Kinsley spoke.

"They were, but still. Does she have no respect for alcohol? I also paid a little visit to that greasy diner you worked at. Also, a dreadful place. By the way, the fat man behind the counter said you're fired."

"I can't believe you went there."

"That's not all. Your ex best friend Krista was my waitress

and your ex-boyfriend was sitting in the booth across from me. I walked over to him, grabbed him by his shirt, and punched him in the face. I told him it was from you." I smiled.

Kinsley covered her mouth in shock.

"You really punched him?"

"I did. You're welcome." I winked.

She wrapped her arms around me and pulled me closer.

"Thank you," she whispered in my ear.

"He hurt you and he wasn't going to get away with it."

Chapter Thirty-Seven

Kinsley

I broke our embrace and placed my hand on one side of his face.

"Are you sure you want this?"

"I'm definitely sure." He smiled. "Are you?" His lips softly brushed against mine.

"Yeah. I'm definitely sure." I brought my lips to his.

I lay in his arms, my head resting against his chest and my body snuggled tightly against his.

"We have to tell my dad," Chase spoke as he stroked my hair.

"I know and I'm not sure how he's going to react because I lied to him."

"Don't worry about that."

"What if he fires me?"

"You're carrying his grandchild. He isn't going to fire you. I think the best place to tell him is at the office."

"Why?" I lifted my head and looked at him. "You don't think

we should do it in private, like at his house?"

"I think we'd be safer at the office. We can tell him and everyone else tomorrow."

"They're all going to be mad we lied to them," I spoke.

"They'll get over it." He kissed the top of my head.

The next morning, I got out of bed and ran to the bathroom.

"Are you okay?" Chase asked as he walked in and held my hair back.

"I'm fine. It's just morning sickness."

"Do you do this every day?" he asked with concern.

"Yes." I vomited again.

"Gee. How long is this going to last?"

"Hopefully only a couple of more weeks," I spoke.

He handed me some tissue to wipe my mouth, and as soon as I stood up, he wrapped his arms around me and held me tight.

"Are you nervous about telling my father?"

"Yes. Very nervous."

"Me too." He grinned as he kissed my forehead.

We drove into the office together and I walked Chase to his office.

"Good morning, Sunshine." He smiled at Lexi.

"Morning, Lexi," I spoke.

She looked at both us with narrowed eyes for she knew something was up.

"Good morning. Did the two of you by chance drive in together?" Her brow raised.

"We did," Chase spoke. "We'll explain later. I'll be down in a bit." He kissed my lips.

"Okay. See you soon." I smiled.

"What the hell is going on?" Lexi exclaimed.

"Like I said, we'll explain later." Chase winked at her.

I walked down the hallway and took a seat at my desk. My nerves were getting the best of me and my legs were starting to shake. I was scared to death to tell Mr. Calloway that I was carrying his grandchild.

"Good morning, Kinsley," he spoke. "Can you come into my office for a minute. I want to go over a couple things with you."

"Good morning, Mr. Calloway." I smiled and nervously followed him into his office.

"Oh good, you're both in here." Chase grinned as he walked in and shut the door.

"Not now, Chase, I'm going over a few things with Kinsley."

"This can't wait, Dad," he spoke as he took the seat next to me and grabbed my hand.

"What the hell is going on?" Mr. Calloway asked as he looked at our hands interlocked.

"You're going to be a grandfather!" Chase blurted out.

"Excuse me?" He cocked his head.

"The baby Kinsley is carrying is mine. Your grandchild."

"What?" He shook his head. "Kinsley told me you weren't the father."

"That's because I told her no one was to ever know. I was in a different place then and I've come to my senses. Kinsley and I are going to have a baby, Dad, and you're just going to have to deal with it."

"I'm so sorry I lied to you, Mr. Calloway."

He sat there behind his desk with his hands cupped together, glaring at the both of us.

"So, the two of you are in a relationship?" he asked.

"I believe we are." Chase smiled at me and I smiled back.

"Thank God." He let out a breath.

"What?" Chase spoke in confusion. "Aren't you going to yell or something?"

"Yell? Why the hell would I yell?" He stood up from his chair with his arms spread wide. "My son is finally in a relationship, and with a woman whom I like very much, and he's going to be a father. This is the best news anyone could ever give me."

"Well." Chase grinned. "I'm happy you're happy."

Mr. Calloway walked over to me, grabbed my hand, and helped me from my chair.

"Welcome to the family, Kinsley." He hugged me.

"We're not getting married, Dad," Chase spoke.

"Doesn't matter, son. Kinsley is carrying my grandchild; that alone makes her family."

He turned to Chase and hugged him.

"Congratulations, son." He patted his back. "We're going to have a celebratory dinner tonight. I can't wait to tell Penelope."

"Thanks, Dad. If it's all right with you, I'm going to steal my girlfriend for a few minutes. We need to tell Lexi."

"Yes, of course. Go." He grinned.

Chase and I walked out of the office and headed down to his.

"Well, he took that better than I thought he would," he spoke.

"I think I'm still in shock." I glanced over at him.

When we approached his office, he asked Lexi to come in.

"For the second time, what the hell is going on?" she asked.

"Kinsley and I are having a baby." Chase grinned as he placed his hand on my belly.

"It's about damn time." She blew out a breath.

"What? You knew?"

Lexi walked over to him and began hitting his arm with her hand.

"Of course I knew, you idiot. Do you think I'm stupid? You really think I believed that Kinsley slept with some random guy? I've been waiting for one of you to come to your senses and tell me."

"I'm sorry, Lexi," I spoke.

"It's not your fault, Kinsley. I know you were doing it to protect this idiot." She began hitting his arm again.

"Will you stop hitting me?" He grabbed her hand.

"Anyway, I suspected the day we had that talk and I told you that you shouldn't be a dad and you got all defensive."

Chapter Thirty-Eight

Chase

I went with Kinsley to her doctor's appointment and heard my baby's heartbeat for the first time. I never expected the overwhelming feeling that came over me. This was really happening and now it was more real than ever. After her appointment, we went back to my house for the night and cooked dinner together.

"Do you like it here?" I asked as I tossed the salad.

"Of course. I love it here. Who wouldn't?" She smiled.

I set down the salad tongs and walked up behind her, wrapping my arms around her waist.

"I want you to move in with me," I whispered as I lightly kissed her ear.

"Really?" She smiled as she turned around and wrapped her arms around my neck.

"Yes. Really. I want me, you, and our child under the same roof. Plus, I have some pretty awesome-sized bedrooms upstairs that would make a great nursery."

"I would love to move in, but I signed a year lease."

"Don't worry about that. I'll take care of your lease."

"That's sweet of you, Chase, but—"

"No buts." I tapped her nose. "You're moving in here. End of discussion."

"If I move in, then all my stuff will be mixed in with yours. I do recall a conversation I overheard where you had a problem with that." She smirked.

"I didn't really have a problem with it. It scared me, that's all. But I'm not scared anymore, Kinsley. I—I love you." The corners of my mouth curved upwards.

"Did it hurt to say that?" she asked with a grin.

"Not at all. In fact, it felt pretty amazing to tell you." I rested my forehead on hers.

"I love you, too, Chase. There's something I want to talk to you about."

"Okay. Let's finish up here and we'll talk over dinner." I kissed her lips.

I set the salad on the table while Kinsley pulled the chicken from the oven. Once we were seated and getting ready to eat, I looked across at her beautiful face.

"What did you want to talk about?"

"I was thinking about taking some business classes." She bit down on her bottom lip.

"Why?"

"I would love to open up an antique shop one day and I feel

I should have some business knowledge."

"I see. An antique shop?"

"When I worked for Mrs. Buckley all those years, I loved it. I loved the timeless pieces and the stories they told."

"I can understand that. Are you going to be able to take some classes with working full time and being pregnant? I don't want you to burn yourself out," I spoke with concern.

"I'll be fine." She smiled.

"Okay, then. Tell me what you need, and I will help you."

"Thank you, but I can do this on my own." She grinned at me.

"But I want to pay for your classes. At least let me do that."

"I have some money saved. Plus, if I'm moving in here, then I won't be paying monthly rent, right?" Her brow arched.

"Oh, my love, you will be paying rent. Just not with money." I grinned.

She took a piece of lettuce from the salad bowl and threw it at me.

****

One Month Later

Kinsley

Every morning before work, Chase and I would head down to the beach. He would surf, and I would do yoga. Delilah was thrilled that he came to his senses and she was happy I moved in with him. She tore up my lease and told me not to worry about the rest of the rent, but Chase wasn't having it. He thanked her for being a good friend to me and paid her the remaining balance of the lease.

After we showered and started getting ready for work, I pulled my black pants from the closet and pulled them on. Shit. I couldn't button them.

"What's wrong?" Chase asked as he saw me struggling.

"These pants don't fit anymore."

He smiled as he walked over to me and placed his hands on my belly.

"You're starting to show, which means you are going to have to go shopping for some maternity clothes. We'll go together after work." He kissed me.

"You have that client dinner tonight with your dad. Did you forget?"

"Shit. I did. I'll cancel."

"No, you won't. This is a very important client and your dad needs you there. I'll ask Lexi if she wants to go shopping."

"Good idea. She'll love to." He smiled. "We should start thinking about the nursery."

"We have time," I spoke.

"We only have five months. What if you deliver early? We need to be ready."

"We'll start talking about it after we find out what we're having," I spoke as I rummaged through the closet trying to find something to wear.

"What? We're finding out?" Chase asked.

"Yes. It'll be easier that way. Don't you want to know what we're having?"

"I guess. I kind of like the suspense, though, of waiting until he or she is actually born."

"Then I'll find out and won't tell you." I smirked.

"And how are you going to keep it from me when we do the nursery? Obviously, if it's a girl, you'll want pink."

"True. Well, it looks like you're finding out with me." I smiled as I straightened his tie.

"And when are we finding out?"

"In three weeks. Lexi wrote it on your calendar already."

"Remind me to thank her," he spoke as he kissed my lips.

****

Chase

"Lexi, come in here, please," I shouted from my desk.

"What's up, boss?" She grinned as she took a seat in front of me.

"Today is the day Kinsley and I find out the gender of baby Calloway."

"I know. How exciting!"

"Something's been bothering me."

"What?" She cocked her head.

"I think Kinsley should tell her mom that she's going to be a grandmother."

"Have you talked to Kinsley about it?" she asked.

"Not yet. I wanted to get your opinion first."

"I don't know, Chase. From what Kinsley told me about her, I'm not sure I'd want her to know if she was my mom. Plus, you met her."

"I know, and believe me, it wasn't a pleasant conversation, but she is her mom and she does have the right to know."

"Tread carefully with this one, my friend. I'm not so sure she'll be open to it."

I sighed as I placed my hands behind my head and leaned back in my chair.

"I just think someday she'll regret not telling her."

"Maybe she will or maybe she won't. That's up to her. Carefully approach her about it and if she starts to get all crazy, drop it immediately."

"Thanks, Lexi." I looked at my watch. "It's time to go find out if I'm having a son or daughter." I grinned as I got up from my desk.

Kinsley and I walked hand in hand into the medical center and took the elevator up to the third floor. Excitement and nervousness overtook me. I didn't care what the baby was, as long as it was healthy. As Kinsley lay down on the bed, I held her hand in anticipation.

"Hello, you two." Dr. Morgan smiled as she entered the room. "Are you ready to see your baby?"

As she placed the transducer on Kinsley's belly, I gulped when I saw a perfectly formed human inside of her. Tears started to fill my eyes as I sat there and stared at the child Kinsley and I created.

"Baby is growing well, and the heartbeat is nice and strong. Do you two want to know the sex?"

Kinsley glanced at me and I gave her a smile and a nod.

"Yes, Dr. Morgan."

"Okay. Let's go down to that area and see what we've got." She smiled.

Instantly, I saw it and my face lit up.

"It's a boy!" I shouted.

"You're right, Mr. Calloway. You're having a boy." Dr. Morgan grinned. "Congratulations."

Kinsley turned to me with tears in her eyes as I gently squeezed her hand.

"We're having a boy." She smiled.

"I love you." I leaned down and kissed her lips.

Chapter Thirty-Nine

Kinsley

I was lying on the bed, on my side, staring at my ultrasound picture, when Chase walked into the bedroom.

"What are you doing?" he asked as he lay next to me, pulled my shirt up, and placed his hand on my belly.

"Staring at our baby." I placed my hand on his. "I can't wait to meet him."

"Me either, sweetheart. There's something I want to talk to you about." He began to softly stroke my belly.

"What is it?"

"I think you should tell your mom about the baby."

"Why would you even say something like that?" I spoke in an irritated tone.

"She has a right to know she's going to be a grandmother."

"Really, Chase?" I sat up and pulled down my shirt. "She doesn't have the right to know anything. She never cared about me. She didn't take care of me. I took care of the both of us. Me!" I shouted as I pointed to myself.

"Baby, calm down," he spoke as he sat up and placed his

hands on my shoulders.

"No, don't tell me what to do! You met her. You saw the environment. For God sakes, she gave you scotch in a plastic cup!"

"Please don't remind me of that. All I'm saying is that she's your mom and she should know. It doesn't mean she has to meet him or anything."

"And what about your mom?" I cocked my head at him. "Don't you think she has a right to know?"

"That's different and you know it. My mother abandoned me."

"And so did mine. She may not have physically abandoned me, but she did emotionally for years. God, I can't even believe you would suggest that!" I got up from the bed, went into the bathroom, and locked the door. I couldn't even look at him, I was so mad.

"Kinsley, please." He fumbled with the door handle. "I'm sorry."

"No, you're not. Obviously, you feel very strongly about it or you wouldn't have mentioned it."

"How long do you intend to stay mad at me?" he asked.

"I don't know yet. Please, just leave me alone."

I closed the lid to the toilet and sat down, placing my face in my hands. Tears started to fill my eyes as I thought about her. I stood up, unlocked the door, and stepped into the bedroom, where Chase was sitting on the edge of the bed. He looked up at me, and instantly, I felt a warmth run through me.

"She never nurtured me. Whenever I'd have nightmares, I would run to her room and call her name. She never responded. She would just moan and roll over. So I'd climb into her bed and snuggle myself against her. She never knew I was there. I hated her for that. I was a child and I needed to be loved. And no matter what, I always took care of her. I cleaned up her vomit, and I cleaned up all her alcohol bottles that were lying all over the house. I resent her for all of it. So I'll be damned if she ever comes near my baby," I cried.

"Damn it, sweetheart. I'm so sorry for even mentioning it," he spoke as he got up from the bed and held me tight. "I'm so sorry. Please don't cry. I should have known better."

"You need to understand that I can't and I won't."

"I do." He held my face in his hands. "I love you."

****

Chase

I sat on my surfboard and stared at Kinsley as she did yoga on her mat in the sand by the shoreline. She was now seven months pregnant and glowing more than ever. She wore baggy low-rise sweatpants and a sports bra, exposing her large belly. She was the most beautiful woman in the world. A smile crossed my lips as I watched her. I was the luckiest man in the world. But I was also a man who was filled with regret. To think that I wanted nothing to do with her or my child revolted me.

"Hey, bro." Steven smiled as he paddled his board up next to mine.

"Hey, Steven."

"Kinsley's looking great. You have what? A couple more

months left until the baby comes?"

"Yeah. It's hard to believe."

"I met someone last night," he spoke.

"Continue?" I smiled.

"Her name is Franny. I ran into her on the street and knocked a bag of groceries out of her hands. Food went flying everywhere."

"I sure hope you helped her pick it up?"

"Of course I did. I'm not that much of an asshole. Anyway, I helped her pick everything up and carried her bags home for her. She only lived a couple of blocks from the store. Damn, Chase. I can't explain it. The feeling I got when I met her."

"You don't have to explain it. I already know the feeling." I smiled.

"We talked for a while and she gave me her phone number. Instead of going to the club last night, I went home and we talked on the phone for hours. I'm taking her to dinner tonight."

"Good for you." I grinned. "It's about time."

"Yeah, well, Alex grew up, you grew up, and I thought maybe it was time I did too. This single life can get lonely at times."

"I know what you mean," I spoke.

Steven and I surfed for a bit, and then it was time to head back and get ready for work.

"I'll see you at the office, bro." I fist-bumped him.

Kinsley bent down and rolled up her yoga mat and then hooked her arm in mine.

"Are you feeling okay?" I asked her.

"I feel great." She smiled as she laid her head on my shoulder.

"How about we leave the office at lunch and go shopping for the nursery? Dad is on a business trip and I'll just have his line transferred over to Lexi."

"I'd love to. But don't forget I have homework tonight that's due tomorrow."

"I know. That's why I suggested we take a half day." I smiled as I kissed the top of her head.

I set my board down in the garage and went inside the house. Kinsley was already in the shower, so I joined her.

"Good thing this shower isn't small or else the three of us wouldn't fit in here." I smirked.

"Are you saying I'm fat, Mr. Calloway?" She grinned as she wrapped her arms around my neck.

"No. But you are taking up a large amount of space." I kissed the tip of her nose.

"Since I'm so large, I guess we won't be having sex anymore." Her brow arched.

"You would never do that. You're hornier than I am, and I didn't think that was possible."

"True." She tilted her head to the side. "I guess I'll just have to think of another punishment for you." She smirked.

Chase Calloway

"Punish away, darling. I look forward to it."

Chapter Forty

Kinsley

"You can build multi-million-dollar programs and computer systems, yet you can't build a simple little crib?" I smirked at him as he sat on the floor with all the pieces scattered around him.

"I don't have to think about computer systems and programs. They come naturally to me. But this—this is ridiculous."

"Hello, anyone home?" I heard Lexi yell from the foyer.

"Upstairs in the baby's room," I shouted.

"Whoa. What's going on in here?" She smiled at me.

"Chase is trying to build the crib."

"Trying?" Her brow arched.

"Listen, Lexi, this isn't as simple as you think it is. This is some complex shit."

"Oh, for God sakes. Give me those directions," she spoke as she walked over to him and ripped them from his hand. "Kinsley, come over here. Chase, leave."

"Excuse me?"

"Me and Kinsley got this. We'll call you when it's done."

"What the hell, Lexi?"

She grabbed Chase by his hand, helped him from the floor, and then pushed him out of the room.

"Go surf some waves or something." She shut the door.

I couldn't help but laugh.

"Are you sure we can do this?" I asked.

"Piece of cake." She grinned.

It took a little over an hour, and finally, the crib was built. It was beautiful and fit for a prince. I walked over to the door and opened it just as Chase was walking up the stairs eating an apple.

"I was just coming to check on the two of you," he spoke.

"It's finished." I smiled.

He stepped inside the room and stared at the crib that sat against the wall.

"How the hell did you build that in an hour?" he asked.

"Girl power, my friend. Girl power." Lexi smiled.

"Thank you." He walked over and kissed Lexi's cheek. "Tell anyone about this and not only will I fire you, but I'll disown you as a best friend."

"Don't worry. I won't tell anyone. I'd hate to embarrass you." She grinned.

"Since you two beautiful ladies worked so hard, how about

I treat you to dinner?" he spoke.

"First of all, it wasn't hard," Lexi said. "And second of all, dinner sounds great. I'm starving."

****

I stood in the middle of the starry-themed nursery and looked around at how perfect it was. Everything was in its place and waiting for the arrival of the prince who was going to occupy it.

"One more week," Chase spoke as his arms wrapped around me from behind.

"I can't believe he's almost here."

"We just need to get through my father's wedding this weekend."

"We'll be fine. First babies are always late."

"Not the answer I wanted to hear." He chuckled.

"That was nice of your dad to postpone their honeymoon until after the baby was born."

"Yeah. He's pretty excited about his grandson. In fact, I think he's more excited than he was about me."

"That's not true." I smacked his hand.

"Are you up for going out to dinner?" he asked. "Or would you rather stay in and we can order something?"

"I would love to go out, and I'm really craving Mediterranean food. Can we go to that place over on Sunset Boulevard?"

"We can go anywhere you want." He kissed my shoulder.

The hostess took us over to a booth, and for some reason, there was barely any room between the seat and the table, so it was impossible for me and my belly to fit.

"Do you have a table?!" I asked with irritation. "Why the hell are your booths like this? God help anyone who is fat."

I heard Chase snicker.

"I'm sorry, ma'am. There's a table right over here," the hostess spoke.

"You think this is funny?" I glared at Chase as we sat down at the table.

"No, darling. Of course I don't." He brought his fist up to his mouth to stop the laughter from escaping him.

"The hell you don't! You wouldn't be laughing."

He reached across the table and grabbed my hand.

"Calm down. It's not you, it's the restaurant. Look around. All the booths seem to be like that. Sweetheart, you're nine months pregnant."

"I know." I sighed. "I just feel like a beached whale."

"You're not a beached whale. You're a stunning and gorgeous woman who's carrying my son. Beached whales are far from being stunning and gorgeous." He smirked.

I couldn't help but laugh.

"I'm sorry," I spoke. "I love you."

"Don't apologize. I love you too."

The Calloway wedding day was here. I stood at the mirror and stared at my large self in my long black strapless Valentino gown. I wasn't feeling too well, but I couldn't let Chase know because it was his father's wedding day and he was the best man. Plus, I didn't want him worrying about me. He had to go over to his father's house early with the other groomsmen, so Lexi and Ben were picking me up.

"You look so beautiful." Lexi smiled as she walked over to me and grabbed my hand.

"Thanks. So do you."

"God, it's hard to believe that little baby Calloway is due to grace us with his presence next week."

"I hope he's on time. I just can't deal with this pregnancy anymore. I'm so uncomfortable."

"Are you ready to go?" she asked.

"As ready as I'll ever be." I smiled.

When we arrived at the church, I saw Chase standing in the hallway talking to Alex. When he glanced over and saw me, a wide grin crossed his face.

"There you are." He walked over and kissed me. "You look absolutely beautiful." He smiled. "How's my son doing?" he asked as he placed his hand on my belly.

"He's fine. How's your dad? Is he nervous?" I asked.

"No. He's a pro at this. I think at this point, it doesn't even faze him."

"Excuse me, Mr. Calloway, we're ready to start now," Belinda the wedding planner spoke to him.

"Alright. I guess it's time. I'll see you soon." He kissed me.

Lexi, Ben, and I walked down the aisle and took our seats in the first row, which was reserved for us by Chase.

"Are you okay?" Lexi asked as she saw me place my hand on my belly.

"I'm fine," I lied.

The truth was, I was having Braxton Hicks, which were making me very uncomfortable. I looked over at Chase, who was standing at the altar next to his dad. He gave me a wink just as the music started and the bride began walking down the aisle. Penelope looked beautiful in her long white satin beaded gown that sat gracefully off her shoulders. Her brown hair was in an up-do with beautiful crystals scattered throughout.

The minister started to speak, and I started to sweat. The pain began to radiate throughout my lower back. Chase knew something was wrong because he kept glancing over at me with a troubled look on his face. I shifted in my seat and Lexi placed her hand on my leg.

"What's wrong?" she asked in a whisper.

"I'm not sure, but I think I'm in labor. Don't say anything yet. I need to get through this ceremony."

"Fuck! Are you serious?"

"I thought they were Braxton Hicks at first, but this is different."

I looked up at Chase, who was staring at me with a narrowed eye, and I lightly shook my head because of the concerned look on his face.

"If anyone can show just cause why this couple cannot lawfully be joined together in matrimony, speak now or forever hold your peace," the minister spoke.

"OH MY GOD!" I shouted uncontrollably.

"Excuse me?" the minister spoke as all eyes diverted to me.

"Holy shit! Sorry." I bit down on my bottom lip as the pain radiated throughout me.

"Baby, what's wrong?" Chase asked as he ran over to me.

"I think I'm in labor."

"Sorry, Dad. I gotta go," he spoke as he placed his hand in his pocket, took out the ring, and handed it to Steven. "Take my place, bro. I need to get Kinsley to the hospital," he spoke as he took hold of both my hands and helped me up from my seat.

Dean walked over to me and kissed my cheek.

"I'm so sorry," I spoke.

"Don't be. This is the best wedding present I could have ever asked for. Go have my grandson and we'll be by later." He smiled.

"Come on, sweetheart. Let's go," Chase spoke as he helped me up the aisle and to the car. I sat there, finally able to breathe. The pain had stopped. Shit. What if it just was Braxton Hicks and I just ruined the wedding? The thought horrified me.

"How are you feeling?" Chase asked as he reached over and

placed his hand on my belly.

"I'm okay now."

"So you're not in labor?" His brow arched.

"I don't know! I've never been in labor before. I can't tell if it's real or not."

As we drove down the highway, the pain shot through me again, jolting me out of my skin.

"FUCK!" I screamed as I placed my hands on my belly. "It's definitely labor!" I yelled.

"We're almost there. Breathe through it. Practice your yoga breathing or something," he spoke in a panicked tone.

The pain subsided as I laid my head back against the headrest and closed my eyes for a moment.

"This is no time for a nap, sweetheart," Chase spoke.

I opened one eye and glared at him.

"I'm not taking a nap!"

He pulled up to the emergency room entrance, threw the car in park, and grabbed a wheelchair from inside the doors. Taking my hand, he helped me from the car and into the chair.

"What's going on?" a tall man in a white coat asked as he approached us.

"She's in labor," Chase calmly spoke.

"It's a good day to have a baby." He smiled. "Did the two of you just come from a wedding?"

"My father's," Chase spoke."

"Are you a doctor?" I asked.

"I'm Dr. Jameson Finn, and you are?"

"Kinsley Davis."

He stopped at the nurses' station inside the ER and told them to call up to Labor and Delivery.

"Tell them that Kinsley Davis is in labor," he spoke.

"They said to keep her down here for now because there aren't any rooms available. But one will be ready soon," the woman in Snoopy scrubs spoke.

"Jesus Christ." Dr. Finn shook his head. "It seems like we have a baby boom going on right now. No worries," he spoke as he wheeled me through the double doors and into an ER room.

"You're kidding me? Right?" Chase spoke with irritation.

"Don't worry. We'll bring her upstairs as soon as a room is ready. I'm going to call and have them send down a labor and delivery nurse. In the meantime, go ahead and change into this lovely gown we had custom made for you." Dr. Finn winked.

Chapter Forty-One

Kinsley

Chase helped me out of my gown and into the hospital one Dr. Finn handed me.

"Any more pain?" Chase asked.

"Not really. It's just uncomfortable."

"Hi there," the tall brunette with the long ponytail spoke. "I'm Kaylee and I'll be your nurse. You must be Kinsley." She smiled at me and then turned to Chase. "Hello." She cocked her head to the side with a grin on her face.

"Hello, darling." Chase smiled back.

I glared at him and he cleared his throat and grabbed my hand. After my exam, I found that I was dilated to four centimeters and Kaylee left the room to order an epidural for me and to call Dr. Morgan."

"What the fuck, Chase?"

"What?"

"You were flirting with the nurse."

"Sweetheart, I wasn't flirting. That's my natural state. You know that."

"THE HELL YOU WEREN'T!" I screamed as another contraction hit.

"Breathe. Breathe. Breathe." His warm breath was in my face.

I did as he told me to, and it didn't help, but eventually the contraction had dissipated.

"Good job, sweetheart." He smiled as he placed his hand on my forehead. "It'll all be over with soon and you'll be holding our son in your arms."

Nurse Kaylee walked in and smiled at Chase. He quickly looked away because he feared for his life.

"Dr. Morgan told me to keep her posted and the anesthesiologist will be here soon to administer your epidural. Is there anything you need?" she asked.

"No."

"And how about you?" She seductively smiled at Chase.

"I would love a cup of coffee." He smiled, and my nails dug into the flesh of his wrist. "So, could you please point me in the direction of the coffee bar?"

"I'll go get you a cup." She grinned. "How do you take it?"

Another contraction hit and this time it almost knocked me out of the bed.

"HE CAN GET HIS OWN FUCKING CUP OF COFFEE!" I yelled through the pain.

"Right. I can get my own. Breathe. Breathe. Breathe." His warm breath swept over me as his face was mere inches from mine.

"STOP TELLING ME TO BREATHE AND GET OUT OF MY FACE!"

"Just sit tight. You'll be pain free soon," Nurse Kaylee spoke as she left the room.

"How's the soon-to-be mom?" Dr. Finn walked in with a smile.

"She's evil," Chase spoke.

Dr. Finn chuckled. "Most women who are in labor are. Trust me. She'll return to normal as soon as she gets the epidural."

"Gee, I hope so," Chase spoke, and I smacked his arm.

"Are you an OB doctor?" I asked him.

"No. I'm actually a neurosurgeon. I'm just helping out in the ER today."

"Fascinating," Chase spoke.

My body filled with excruciating pain as I gripped Chase's hand. He didn't say a word and I appreciated it.

"It'll be over within a minute, Kinsley. Just focus on your breathing. Deep breath in, deep breath out," Dr. Finn spoke.

After the contraction subsided and Dr. Finn left the room, Chase narrowed his eye at me.

"It's okay for him to tell you to breathe, yet you yell at me to stop?"

"Do you really want to discuss this now? Really, Chase? Because I do believe I'll win."

Before he had a chance to speak, the anesthesiologist walked in and gave me my epidural.

"That should start kicking in, in about ten to thirty minutes." The anesthesiologist smiled.

"I'm rooting for ten," Chase spoke.

****

Chase

Six hours later, our son, Christopher Chase Calloway, came into the world at 7lbs 3 oz. After Kinsley got her epidural, it was smooth sailing. The moment he was born, tears of happiness filled my eyes.

"He's beautiful." I kissed Kinsley's forehead as she held him in her arms.

"He looks like you." She smiled at me.

"Of course he does. He's a Calloway." I smirked.

Kinsley and I took an hour and bonded with him before I had to make numerous phone calls to family and friends. I couldn't stop staring at him. He was so tiny and perfect.

"Do you want to hold your son?" Kinsley asked.

"I'm kind of afraid. I've never held a baby before."

"You'll know what to do." She smiled as she handed him over to me.

As I stared at him, guilt resided inside me. If I hadn't come to my senses, I wouldn't be here, holding this little life that we created. Kinsley changed me and the love I felt for her and him was overwhelming. He was my son and the thought that I was so close to not being a part of his life frightened me.

****

Two Months Later

"Is he all set to go?" I asked Kinsley as I walked into the nursery.

"He sure is. Everything you need is in the diaper bag. Are you sure about this, Chase?"

"I'm positive. He'll be fine. Don't worry." I kissed her lips. "Have a good day at school."

"I'll be by to pick him up after my classes."

"I'll see you later, darling. Are you ready, slugger?" I smiled at him as I picked up the car seat and took it to the car.

Kinsley's classes started back up today and I didn't want my son being raised by nannies or babysitters, so he came to work with me. Kinsley didn't think it was a good idea, but I did. Plus, I knew my father would be thrilled to see him.

"Good morning, sunshine." I smiled at Lexi as I stopped at her desk.

"Oh my God, Christopher." She jumped out of her chair and took him from his car seat.

"Again, good morning, sunshine," I spoke.

"Yeah. Yeah. Good morning."

I sighed as I went into my office and set the car seat and diaper bag on the couch.

"Don't forget you have a meeting at noon with Castle Corp," Lexi spoke in between cooing at Christopher.

"Shit. I did forget. Thanks for reminding me. Now please hand over my son so I can take him to see his grandfather."

"Do I have to?" Lexi pouted.

I stood there and cocked my head at her.

"Fine." She put him in my arms.

I walked down to my father's office and opened his door.

"Knock, knock. Someone came to see you," I spoke as I stepped inside.

"Well, hello there, Christopher, come to Grandpa." He smiled as he got up from his desk and took him from me. "Did Kinsley start school today?"

"Yeah. She did. Can I talk to you for a minute, Dad?"

"Sure, son. Sit down," he spoke as he took a seat behind his desk with Christopher. "What's on your mind?"

"I'm going to ask Kinsley to marry me."

"Well, look at you. My son is growing up." He smirked. "I wondered how long it was going to take you."

"I've been wanting to ask her for the past few months, but with her being pregnant, her hands and fingers were swollen, and I didn't want to give her the ring if she couldn't wear it. She was very self-conscious towards the end. Then Christopher was born and it's been a little crazy."

"I understand. When are you going to ask her?"

"Tomorrow night. Lexi and Ben are going to watch Christopher while we go out. What if she says no, Dad? I'll admit I'm a little scared."

"She won't, son. Kinsley loves you. You have nothing to worry about."

Chapter Forty-Two

Kinsley

Chase and I bathed Christopher and put him down to sleep. I had homework that I needed to do, but I wanted to spend time with Chase before I started it. I hadn't seen him all day except when I picked up the baby and I missed him. I snuggled up against him on the couch as he held me in his strong arms. We talked about our day and watched a movie together. Christopher's timing was impeccable because as soon as the movie ended, he woke up and wanted to be fed.

"I'll give him his bottle," Chase spoke as he kissed my head. "You go start your homework."

"Are you sure? I can feed him."

"Sweetheart, go do your homework. I've got this." He smiled as he kissed my lips.

I went into the kitchen to get the bottle ready while Chase went upstairs and took Christopher from his crib. When he came down, he took a seat on the couch and I handed him his bottle.

"Thank you. I love you." I smiled.

"I love you too. I'll be up when he's done eating."

Chase Calloway

I went upstairs, changed into my nightshirt, grabbed my laptop, and sat down on the bed. Shit. I forgot my book on the kitchen table. As I was walking down the stairs, I heard Chase talking to Christopher. He was already an amazing father, and every time I saw him with our son, my heart melted. I took a seat on the steps and listened for a few moments before going down and grabbing my book.

"Your dad needs to have a little talk with you," he spoke. "Your mom is an amazing woman, but you already know that. I see the way you look at her. I look at her that way too. You can't help but to fall in love with her. She's smart, kind, selfless and the most beautiful woman in the world. She truly has the soul of an angel. She's the strongest woman I know, and she puts up with me, even though there are times where I wouldn't put up with me. When we first met, I knew right away she was special. She was unlike any woman I'd ever met, and to be honest, it frightened the hell out of me. The more I was around her, the more in love with her I fell. She opened my eyes to what life really should be. See, Christopher, I was too afraid to love anyone, and she changed all that. I'm going to ask her to marry me because there's nothing in this world I want more than to call her my wife. I'm really nervous; I won't lie to you, little buddy. I'm so afraid that your mom, this magnificent woman who deserves everything in the entire world, isn't ready or will say no. Neither one of us has ever brought up marriage. Maybe the thought never even crossed her mind. She seems content with the way things are and that's what worries me. I love her so much and even if she says she's not ready yet, it won't change a thing, because I will wait an entire lifetime until she is. You'll see what I'm talking about when you get to know her better. You're very lucky to have her as your mom. This stays between us, okay?"

Tears started to stream down my face and my heart broke knowing that he was afraid I wasn't ready to marry him and that I might say no. I couldn't go down there, so I went back to our room and waited for him to come up.

"He's all fed, changed, and fast asleep." Chase smiled as he walked into the bedroom, climbed on the bed, and gave me a kiss.

"Thank you." I smiled.

"I'm going to go grab my laptop from downstairs. I have some work to do as well. Do you need anything while I'm down there?"

"My book that's on the kitchen table. Also, bring up a bottle of wine and a couple of glasses." I smiled.

"Sounds good. I'll be right back." He winked.

Chase Calloway wasn't just my baby's father. He was the man of my dreams and I never knew I could love someone so much as I did him. A few moments later, he walked back into the bedroom and set the bottle of wine and glasses on the nightstand.

"Want me to pour some now?" he asked.

"How about we wait a little bit?"

"Just let me know when you're ready for it."

He stripped out his clothes and slipped into a pair of navy blue pajama bottoms. He climbed on the bed, rested his laptop on his legs, and began working.

"Chase?" I spoke as I set my laptop over to the side.

"Yeah, baby," he answered as he stared at his computer screen, typing away.

"I love you."

"I love you too, sweetheart."

"Will you marry me?" I blurted out.

His fingers came to a standstill as he slowly turned his head and our eyes met.

"What?" he asked as a shocked expression splayed across his handsome face.

"Will you marry me? If you're not ready, I'll understand."

He closed the lid to his laptop and set it on the floor.

"I am so ready to marry you." He jumped off the bed, went into the closet and returned with a small blue velvet box. "I was going to ask you to marry me." He flipped open the lid. "But I was afraid you weren't ready."

"Oh my God, Chase. It's beautiful." I placed my right hand over my mouth as I stared at the three-carat princess-cut white-gold diamond ring.

With a smile on his face, he took the ring from the box and held it up in front of me.

"Let me do this. Kinsley Davis, I love you with all my heart and soul. Will you marry me, darling?"

"Yes, Chase Calloway, I will marry you." I smiled as tears filled my eyes.

He took hold of my left hand and slipped the ring on my

finger.

"I promise to love you for eternity. I can't imagine my life without you," he spoke as he leaned in and kissed my lips.

I wrapped my arms around his neck and placed my forehead against his.

"And I promise to love you for eternity."

Chapter Forty-Three

Four Months Later

Kinsley

"Hello, my sweet boy." I smiled as I picked up Christopher from his crib. "Did you have a good nap?"

He smiled and laid his head on my shoulder. After changing his diaper, I walked downstairs and the doorbell rang. With Christopher in my arms, I opened the door and stood there in shock.

"Jimmy?"

"Kinsley. You are one hard woman to find," he spoke.

"My God. What are you doing here?"

"I need to talk to you about your mother."

"Come in." I opened the door wider.

"Who's this handsome little guy?" He smiled.

"This is Christopher, my son."

"Your son?" he asked in shock. "Wow. It's good to see you." He reached out and touched my arm.

"It's good to see you too. How did you find me?"

"I hired a private investigator. I had no choice. I needed to find you. Your mom is in the hospital, Kinsley, and she's asking to see you. She's dying, and she doesn't have much time left." He lowered his head.

Suddenly, I felt weak, so I sat down on the couch.

"What's wrong with her?" I asked.

"Her liver is failing."

Tears started to fill my eyes as I looked up at the ceiling.

"I'm not surprised," I softly spoke.

"Listen, Kinsley, I know she was a shit mother, but she's still your mom and she wants to see her daughter before she dies."

Christopher started to cry, so I got up from the couch and put him in his high chair.

"I need to give him his dinner," I spoke as I grabbed the baby food from the cabinet.

"How old is he?" Jimmy asked.

"Six months."

I heard the front door open, and when Chase walked into the kitchen, he stopped dead in his tracks.

"Umm. What's going on here?" he asked.

"Chase, this is Jimmy, from back home. Jimmy, this is my fiancé, Chase Calloway."

"Nice to meet you, man," Jimmy spoke as he extended his

hand.

"Ah yes, I do believe Kinsley has mentioned you." Chase shook his hand. "What brings you to California?"

"Kinsley can tell you. I need to get going. It was good to see you." He smiled at me. "Thanks for taking care of her." He turned to Chase. "You have a beautiful family."

"Thank you," Chase spoke.

As soon as he left, I sat down at the table and began feeding Christopher.

"Are you going to tell me what that was all about?" he asked.

"My mom is dying of liver failure and she's asking to see me."

"Oh, baby." He walked over and kissed the top of my head. "I'm sorry."

"I always knew this day would come. To be honest, I'm surprised it took this long with the amount of alcohol she drank every day."

"I'll feed Christopher," he spoke as he placed his hand on mine.

I jerked away.

"I can feed my son," I shouted in an irritated tone.

"Sweetheart, talk to me."

"I don't want to talk about anything, Chase. So just drop it," I snapped.

"Okay, fine. I'm going upstairs to change."

As soon as I was finished feeding Christopher, I took him upstairs and handed him to Chase.

"Can you bathe him, please? I need some fresh air."

"Of course. Come on, little man, let's get you cleaned up."

I went downstairs, grabbed a blanket and a bottle of wine, and took it down to the beach. Darkness was falling upon the sky and the stars were waiting patiently to make their appearance. Sitting down on the blanket, I brought the bottle to my lips and took a sip as I stared out into the ocean water.

"You okay?" Chase asked as he sat down beside me and brought his knees up to his chest.

"I'm sorry for snapping at you. To be honest, I don't know if I'm okay or not."

"It's okay, sweetheart. You're going through a lot of mixed emotions right now." He hooked his arm around me and I laid my head on his shoulder.

"A part of me hates her and a part of me loves her."

"We'll go to Indiana. You have to make peace with her, Kinsley. If you don't, you'll end up regretting it the rest of your life."

"I know."

"You can do this, baby, and Christopher and I will be there for you. I'll make a few calls, get a private jet, and we'll go first thing tomorrow morning."

"Then I guess we better get packing," I spoke as I took a sip of wine.

"By the way, you never really did tell me who that Jimmy guy is?"

"He's her cousin. He gave up on her a long time ago. They had a huge fight one night and he never came around again. He owns a car repair shop in town. He buys vintage cars and rebuilds them."

"Come on, let's go inside. I have calls to make and we need to get things ready to leave tomorrow," he spoke.

****

When we arrived in Indiana, we checked into a hotel because I knew the house was going to be filthy and I didn't want Christopher there. As soon as we settled in, we headed straight to the hospital.

"You can do this, sweetheart. You're a strong woman," Chase spoke as he reached over and held my hand.

"I know."

As we entered the hospital, the sick feeling in my belly intensified. Chase held Christopher in one hand and held mine with the other. I didn't think I could do this without him here and I was so grateful for all his support. We took the elevator up to the second floor and walked down the hallway until we found room 2101. I stopped in the doorway and took in a deep breath as Chase gave my hand a gentle squeeze. I slowly walked into the room and my mom turned her head and looked at me. A small, weak smile graced her face when she saw me.

"Kinsley," she spoke in a soft voice.

"Hi, Mom," I spoke as I walked over to her bed. "I want you to meet my fiancé Chase Calloway and your grandson,

Christopher."

Tears filled her eyes as she looked at him.

"My grandson? You're a mother?"

"Yeah." I smiled.

"I met him already." She looked at Chase.

"Hi. I apologize for being rude," Chase spoke.

"Nah. Don't be. You didn't tell me anything I already didn't know. Can I hold my grandson?"

"Of course," I spoke.

Chase walked over and put Christopher in her arms. Tears ran down her face as she held him against her.

"You're so handsome," she spoke to him.

After a few moments, Christopher started to cry, so I took him from her and handed him to Chase.

"He's probably hungry," I spoke.

"I'll go feed him and leave you two alone."

Chase walked out of the room and I took a seat in the chair and stared at my mother. She was so frail and weak.

"How long have you known, Mom?" I asked.

"I kind of suspected something was going on the past couple of years."

"You could have gotten help. You could have asked me to help you," I spoke.

"You've helped me enough, Kinsley. I didn't want to put that on you. You had Henry and you were doing your own thing."

"It doesn't matter." I shook my head.

"Listen to me. I know I was a shit mother, but I loved you and I did what I did for you. I needed you to be stronger than I ever was. I'm sorry, Kinsley. I'm so sorry." She began to cry.

Suddenly, all the anger I felt for her all these years slowly dissipated away. This woman, whom I called my mom, was dying and remaining angry at her for something neither she or I could change wouldn't solve anything. She needed my forgiveness.

"I forgive you, Mom." I squeezed her hand. "I am strong and it's because of you."

I got up from my chair and wrapped my arms around her as we both cried together. After we settled down, we talked for a while. I told her all about California and how I was going to school. I shared my dream of owning my own antique shop and she told me for the first time in my life that she was proud of me. After Chase was finished feeding Christopher, he came back into the room and we stayed for a while longer so she could spend some time with her grandson. She was tired and growing weaker every minute we were there.

"We better go and let you get some rest," I spoke.

"Thanks for coming, Kinsley," my mother whispered.

"I love you, Mom." I leaned over and gave her a hug. "We'll be back tomorrow morning."

"I love you too."

Later that night, Jimmy called me at the hotel and told me that my mother had passed away.

"I'm sorry, sweetheart," Chase spoke as he held me tight.

"She's in a better place now," I cried on his shoulder. "She doesn't have to suffer anymore."

A couple days later, we buried her in the same cemetery my father was buried at.

"Kinsley." I felt a hand on my shoulder.

"Well, well." Chase smiled. "If it isn't the waitress from that grease pit."

I turned around and locked eyes with Krista.

"I'm sorry about your mom."

"Thanks, Krista. I appreciate it."

"I didn't know you had a baby. He's so sweet." She smiled.

"He is." I hooked my arm around Chase. "They both are and they're both the love of my life, so thank you."

"For what?" she asked.

"For sleeping with Henry. Because if you hadn't, I'd probably still be stuck in this miserable town, living a miserable life with a man I never even loved. But thanks to you, I moved to California and met this wonderful man and had this beautiful baby."

"Umm. You're welcome?"

I gave her a smile and gracefully walked away.

Chapter Forty-Four

Sixteen Years Later

Chase

It was hard to believe that Kinsley and I had been married sixteen years already. It seemed like it was yesterday when I first laid eyes on her. The three of us turned into the five of us. Christopher was almost seventeen, and the twins, Chanel and Camille, were blooming teenagers at the age of thirteen. My father retired a few years back and I stepped in and took over the company. Christopher was following in my footsteps, not only attending Stanford, but he would be the next generation to take over Calloway Tech. The girls were typical teens, and they were smart, strong, and beautiful like their mother. Needless to say, when we found out we were having twins, we were shocked. Kinsley didn't know that twins ran in her family. So after some investigating of the family tree, we found out that Kinsley's great-grandmother was a twin.

After Kinsley graduated from college, I gave her her dream and she became the proud owner of an antique shop she called Timeless Treasures, which turned a profit in the first year. I was so proud of her and fell in love with her even more.

"Listen, sweetheart, I don't know what's going on yet. I'll text you as soon as I find out. I have to go," Christopher spoke as he walked into the kitchen.

"Who was that?" I asked him.

"Hold on." He put up his finger as his phone rang again. "Emily, darling, I was just going to call you. Was that tonight? Ugh. I'm so sorry, but I completely forgot. My parents had me busy all day doing work for them. I'm afraid tonight won't work, so let's set something up within the next couple days. Great, gotta run, my mom's yelling for me."

Kinsley and I looked at each other as Christopher made another call.

"Hey, baby, it's me. "I'll pick you up around eight o'clock. Can't wait to see you either."

"What the hell is going on?" Kinsley asked him.

"What?" He shrugged.

"Obviously, our son is juggling two girls at once."

"Three, Dad. Emily, Katia, and Val."

"Oh." A grin crossed my face. "Three girls." I glanced over at Kinsley.

"And you think that's okay?" she asked Christopher.

"Why not? It's not like I'm in a relationship with any of them. It's all casual dating."

"And you think just because you're 'casual dating,' it's okay to lie? Are you having sex with all of them?" Kinsley spoke sternly as she pointed her finger at him.

"Mom! Oh my God!"

"Don't you oh my God me, Christopher Chase Calloway! Chase, talk to him!"

I sighed as I hooked my arm around him.

"Listen, son, believe me when I tell you, this will all catch up to you, and when it does, it's not going to be pretty. Just be honest from the beginning with these girls, and if you're having sex, you better be using a condom."

"And, Chase?" Kinsley spoke.

"And you better make sure the girl is on birth control as well. If she's not, double up the glove." I winked.

"Dad, come on."

"Your father and I used a condom and it broke," Kinsley spoke. "And then came you." Her brow arched.

"Okay. Okay, I get it. Do you realize how awkward it is talking to you about this?" Christopher spoke.

"I can only imagine, son. Now go have your date and be safe."

Christopher started to walk out of the kitchen and Kinsley stopped him.

"Christopher." She pointed to her cheek.

He walked over and gave her a kiss.

"I love you, Mom."

"I love you too." She smiled.

As soon as he left the kitchen, I walked over to Kinsley and wrapped my arms around her, pulling her into me.

"He can't help it, sweetheart. He's a Calloway and we Calloway men are natural born charmers."

****

I was looking out the window at my beautiful family on the beach before I headed down to join them. Christopher was charming his way into the heart of yet another girl and Chanel and Camille were in the water with Kinsley. I smiled at what a lucky man I truly was. This was something I never envisioned for myself. I was nothing but a man who hid behind fear. Then Kinsley came along and changed all that. She set me free and I would never stop loving her.

I stepped out onto the patio, grabbed my surfboard, and ran down to the beach.

"Surf's up, son. Let's go!" I smiled as I ran past him.

"Sure thing, Dad. I'm right behind you!" He grabbed his board and followed behind.

I set my surfboard in the water and paddled up to Kinsley.

"I love you." I leaned over and kissed her.

"I love you too." She smiled.

About the Author

Sandi Lynn is a New York Times, USA Today and Wall Street Journal bestselling author who spends all her days writing. She published her first novel, Forever Black, in February 2013 and hasn't stopped writing since. Her addictions are shopping, going to the gym, romance novels, coffee, chocolate, margaritas, and giving readers an escape to another world.

Be a part of my tribe!

Facebook: www.facebook.com/Sandi.Lynn.Author
Twitter: www.twitter.com/SandilynnWriter
Website: www.authorsandilynn.com
Pinterest: www.pinterest.com/sandilynnWriter
Instagram: www.instagram.com/sandilynnauthor
Goodreads: http://bit.ly/2w6tN25
My Shop: www.sandilynnromance.com

If you're interested in purchasing a signed paperback from me, click on the "My Shop" link above!

Printed in Great Britain
by Amazon